Man For Me

Also From Laurelin Paige

Man in Charge Duet
Man in Charge
Man in Love

Slay Series
Slay One: Rivalry
Slay Two: Ruin
Slay Three: Revenge
Slay Four: Rising
Slash: A Slay Novella

The Fixed Series
Fixed on You
Found in You
Forever with You
Hudson
Falling Under You: A Fixed Trilogy Novella (1001 Dark Nights)
Chandler
Dirty, Filthy Fix: A Fixed Trilogy Novella (1001 Dark Nights)
Fixed Forever

Dirty Universe
Dirty Filthy Rich Boys
Dirty Filthy Rich Men
Dirty Filthy Rich Love
Dirty, Sexy Player
Dirty Sexy Games
Sweet Liar
Sweet Fate
Dirty Sweet Valentine
Wild Rebel
Wild War
Wild Heart

Found Duet
Free Me
Find Me

First and Last
First Touch
Last Kiss

Hollywood Heat
Sex Symbol
Star Struck
One More Time
Close

Co-Written Works:
Written with Sierra Simone:
Porn Star
Hot Cop

Written with Kayti McGee:
Dating Season
Spring Fling
Summer Rebound
Fall Hard
Winter Bloom
Spring Fever
Summer Lovin

Miss Match
Love Struck
MisTaken: A Novella

Man For Me

A Man In Charge Novella

By Laurelin Paige

1001 DARK NIGHTS
PRESS

Man For Me
A Man In Charge Novella
By Laurelin Paige

1001 Dark Nights
Copyright 2021 Laurelin Paige
ISBN: 978-1-951812-57-7

Foreword: Copyright 2014 M. J. Rose

Published by 1001 Dark Nights Press, an imprint of Evil Eye Concepts, Incorporated

Sign up for the 1001 Dark Nights Newsletter
and be entered to win a Tiffany Key necklace.

There's a contest every month!

Go to www.1001DarkNights.com to subscribe.

**As a bonus, all subscribers can download
FIVE FREE exclusive books!**

Dedication

-for my husband,
who I fell in love with while scheming to get the wrong man

One Thousand and One Dark Nights

Once upon a time, in the future…

*I was a student fascinated with stories and learning.
I studied philosophy, poetry, history, the occult, and
the art and science of love and magic. I had a vast
library at my father's home and collected thousands
of volumes of fantastic tales.*

*I learned all about ancient races and bygone
times. About myths and legends and dreams of all
people through the millennium. And the more I read
the stronger my imagination grew until I discovered
that I was able to travel into the stories... to actually
become part of them.*

*I wish I could say that I listened to my teacher
and respected my gift, as I ought to have. If I had, I
would not be telling you this tale now.
But I was foolhardy and confused, showing off
with bravery.*

*One afternoon, curious about the myth of the
Arabian Nights, I traveled back to ancient Persia to
see for myself if it was true that every day Shahryar
(Persian: شهريار, "king") married a new virgin, and then
sent yesterday's wife to be beheaded. It was written
and I had read that by the time he met Scheherazade,
the vizier's daughter, he'd killed one thousand
women.*

Something went wrong with my efforts. I arrived in the midst of the story and somehow exchanged places with Scheherazade — a phenomena that had never occurred before and that still to this day, I cannot explain.

Now I am trapped in that ancient past. I have taken on Scheherazade's life and the only way I can protect myself and stay alive is to do what she did to protect herself and stay alive.

Every night the King calls for me and listens as I spin tales. And when the evening ends and dawn breaks, I stop at a point that leaves him breathless and yearning for more. And so the King spares my life for one more day, so that he might hear the rest of my dark tale.

As soon as I finish a story... I begin a new one... like the one that you, dear reader, have before you now.

Chapter One

Starting an evening with an orgasm should have been a sign of more good things to come. Literally.

Of course, most orgasms aren't given out of pity, and this one definitely was. Even if Scott hadn't so much as said that directly, it was a big clue when he dismissed me just when it was his turn for the hand job.

His cutting remark echoed in my head: *"Only reason I got you off was so that you'd leave me alone."*

I refused to cry as I stomped away from him.

Well, stomped until I got to the edge of the roof. There, my departure became more awkward as I attempted to descend the steel ladder to the main rooftop level with as much poise as a woman dressed in a cocktail dress could muster. Which is to say, not any poise at all. Mostly, I tried to keep my knees together so that no one below could see that my panties had gone the way of my dignity—stuffed into Scott Sebastian's pocket.

Not *my* cocktail dress, I should add—borrowed from my older sister, as all my formal attire was—which meant that the snag that I got halfway down the damn thing would have to be repaired before I returned it. There went next week's Café A Lot money.

Fuck everything.

Rather, fuck everything but Scott Sebastian, the only thing I actually wanted to be fucking at the moment.

At the bottom of the ladder, I sent one more angry glare toward the upper roof, hoping that my sometimes lover would be standing there to see it.

Alas, the glare went unreceived.

And I, in a dramatic flare that no one was there to witness, lifted my chin and stormed over to the bar.

"Everything going well?" I asked the bartender as I slipped behind the counter. His name was Denim.

Denim.

I'd be appalled at his parents for giving him such a ridiculous name if I wasn't so sure that it was a name change he'd taken for himself.

Actors.

Correction: *Millennial actors.* The other actors weren't quite so eccentric.

The city was full of them moonlighting as waitstaff, and since my job description as receptionist somehow included every random task not otherwise assigned in the PR department, I was frequently the point person for the service staff at parties such as this.

Obviously, I wasn't the best at this part of my job, since I'd been getting busy with my boss instead of remaining in sight and available. But honestly, I would have been overjoyed to have this particular task doled out to someone else. I'd frequently asked for just that over the last few years, only to have my request put off time and time again. So now this was just another thing in my life that could fuck right off.

"Peachy," Denim said flatly, and charming as he wasn't, I didn't take it upon myself to manage him the way some others in my position might have.

I hadn't really come by to check up on him.

He eyed me as I rooted around in his wine fridge. "Anything I can get for you, Ms. Waters?"

"Nah. I got it." I pulled out an already opened, mostly full Moet & Chandon and made sure the Nectar Imperial flavor was a demi-sec—it was—and then shut the fridge door with my hip. I held up the bottle for Denim to see. "A guest requested this."

Never mind that the guest was me and that I wasn't really a guest.

"Do you need some flutes?"

"Nope! I'm good."

"Ah, so that's the kind of evening this is going to be," said another familiar voice as I slipped back to the other side of the bar.

I turned to see the only other face I wanted to see at the moment—really, the only other face I wanted to see at most moments.

"That's the kind of evening this already *is*, Brett," I whined, the way a girl does when she's having a bad time and she sees the person who knows her better than anyone else in the world.

He frowned as he used his thumb to clean up my smudged mascara.

"Want me to beat him up?"

I forced myself not to shiver at his touch. "Yes, please."

"On it."

He smiled, and the bright white of his teeth somehow managed to accentuate the green of his eyes. It was hard to know where to look, which was often the case. Every part of his face was attractive, from his dimpled chin to his chiseled cheekbones to his thick eyebrows to the scruff covering his angled jawline.

Hands down, he was the hottest man I knew. Even after years of knowing him, I wasn't immune to his looks. The only reason I hadn't chased after him was because he wasn't running. If I wanted him in my bed, I had a feeling he'd follow me like a lost puppy. That was his only problem—which wasn't really a problem in general, just where my libido was concerned—he adored me, and f'd up broken girl that I was, I required a certain degree of assholery to turn me on.

Scott Sebastian, case in point.

Of course Brett wouldn't really beat Scott up because A) he wouldn't hurt a fly, B) Scott was his boss as well as mine, and C) Scott was his cousin—relevance in that order—but it was a nice sentiment all the same.

I held up the bottle. "I'm going to drown my misery with expensive champagne that I didn't pay for. Want to join me?"

Brett peered over one shoulder than the other. "I can't. I think I need to schmooze a little longer."

See? Brett was one of the good ones. He wouldn't even try to talk me out of shirking my own duties, despite the fact that he had gotten me the job and held rank over me.

Since I was not one of the good ones, it wasn't beneath me to try to change his mind. "You're tucked in the corner by the bar with me. You're already not schmoozing."

"Well, I'm also trying to hide from Adrienne Thorne."

I threw my head back and groaned, for his sake as well as mine. The blue-haired sexagenarian called the office at least once a week trying to land an appointment with Brett. His personal assistant had stopped taking her calls, and so she'd started calling the main line, meaning I was now the one making up excuses for why Brett couldn't see her. "You should just tell her we're never going to work with her and get it over with."

"I have, Eden. Several times. She thinks she can change my mind."

Because Brett was so nice that being dumped by him probably felt like an invitation to try harder to win him.

Poor guy. He couldn't help being good-natured.

"Want *me* to beat *her* up?" I smoothed my hand down his tie, more to cop a feel than to straighten it.

Yeah, he wasn't the guy for me, but he had a great body. Sue me for appreciating it.

I silently scored myself a point when he shivered. "I'm afraid you'd really do it, even if I said yes in jest."

"I mean, it would probably cost me my job."

A beat passed before we broke into laughter. Whether or not Scott Sebastian returned my affection, sleeping with the boss gave me the advantage. I'd one hundred percent been the one who'd gone after him, but the Sebastians were concerned enough about their image that they'd think twice before letting me go. And if I did get fired, I'd likely leave with a hefty paycheck.

Not that I'd ever accuse the guy of anything, but as long as he thought I might, and the possibility gave me job security, I wasn't going to admit that I wouldn't.

Thinking about my job gave me a second to consider sticking around like I was supposed to and helping Brett hide from Adrienne Thorne, for no other reason but that I liked his company, and he always cheered me up after Scott broke my heart.

But the notion was quickly dismissed when I saw the devil himself climb down the ladder and casually throw my panties in a trash can. Naturally, he hadn't snagged anything, and he looked just as put together as he had when he'd gone up.

Fuck him, fuck him, fuck him.

Brett followed my eyeline and stiffened when he saw what I was looking at. *Who* I was looking at.

Maybe he really would beat Scott up. If I asked him to.

I *wouldn't* ask him to. I hated myself already for making Brett feel like he had to choose sides. Which didn't stop me from returning to Scott time and time again like a beat-up boomerang, but it did compel me to defuse the current situation with distance.

As in, me distancing myself from the object of my affection before I ended up back at his side.

"Anyway"—I patted Brett's chest like I was calming a ferocious guard dog—"you do that work stuff, I'll be on the other side of the roof." I nodded to the area at the far end of the party that had been roped off to store the extra boxes of alcohol so that the staff didn't have to go inside when they ran out of vodka or scotch. I'd noticed a couch over there during setup, and right now the secluded spot was calling my name. "Join me later?"

"Yep." I didn't miss the longing that flashed through his eyes, as it did on occasion, but as always, I didn't acknowledge it. He gestured to my champagne. "Save me some."

"Sure." I managed not to roll my eyes. He pretended he wasn't blue blood because he wasn't as blue blooded as Scott's branch of the Sebastian tree, but he'd grown up much more dignified than I had and preferred a dry wine to my dessert liquors.

Still, he'd drink it when he joined me. Whether to show his support or because he didn't want me to drink it all alone and get wasted, I didn't know.

Whichever his reason, I made sure to grab another bottle before taking off to solitude. It was early in the night, and I'd already been dumped by Scott. Again. I was not in the mood to have my drinking limited.

Chapter Two

I ignored two texts from my sister and her first phone call. When my dumb ass had grabbed the second bottle of champagne, I hadn't made sure it was opened, and I couldn't pop a cork for the life of me. After accidentally spilling half of the first bottle—yeah, it had been a night—I wasn't drunk enough to deal with her.

But persistent witch that she was, she then did the call-let-it-ring-hang-up-immediately-call-again thing, and finally I'd been annoyed into answering. "What?"

"Did you get my message?"

"No, I'm working." I mean, I was supposed to be working. She didn't know that I wasn't.

She made that sound that said she was as annoyed with me as I was with her, which only annoyed me more. "I need you to pick up some diapers on your way home."

No *please*. No *Can you*. Just *do*.

I threw my head back and stared at the night sky, reminding myself I was in no position to be shitty to her since she currently let me live with her in her snazzy prime real estate Midtown location for a rent price that couldn't be matched in the far reaches of the state. "How the fuck can you be out of diapers? You always get more than you need."

I reminded myself not to be shitty. Didn't mean I listened.

"I left a pack at the daycare today, and when I opened the one left at home tonight, I realized Nolan picked up a size for three-year-olds rather than size three. I didn't even know they made them that size. Who even still has their three-year-old in diapers? I had to use duct tape to keep it on

Finch. I could barely get his pajamas on over it. Poor thing looks like a bloated burrito."

I smiled at the image of my nephew her words had conjured.

Then immediately frowned. Maybe if Avery wasn't such a judgmental perfectionist, I'd feel more kindly toward her. She was probably berating herself for not being more prepared and screaming at Nolan for making the mistake in the first place. She needed a calm, understanding, supportive voice right now.

Obviously, she wasn't going to get that from me. "Why can't you send Nolan to get them? He's the one who messed up."

"He's already asleep."

I pulled my phone away from my ear to look at the time. It was barely ten. The guy was such a lightweight.

No, that wasn't fair. My sister's husband worked his ass off. It was his corporate salary that provided for my housing, and his generosity in letting me stay with him. Honestly, besides Finch, Nolan was my favorite thing about my sister. If it weren't for him, I never would have met Brett. He'd been Nolan's best man at their wedding a decade ago, and in my job as maid of honor, the two of us had been tasked with planning a lot of the activities together.

We'd hit it off so well, and with Nolan wrapped up in his new circle of married-with-kids friends, nowadays Brett was closer to me than his former college buddy.

"Eden, just…" Avery let out a sigh of frustration. "Could you not be a bitch and just pick up the damn diapers? You're already out. There's no reason you can't pick some up on your way home."

What if I'm not planning on coming home?

It was what I wanted to say.

I held my tongue because, considering the mood Avery was in, she would likely rub in the fact that, even when Scott was into me, he rarely let me sleep over, and that was a truth I was already facing head on. I definitely didn't need my flawless, amazing sister with the flawless, amazing life rubbing it in.

Flawless except for the right diaper size, anyway.

I took the final swig of champagne, which was really more like a sip, and gritted my teeth. "Fine. I'll pick up your damn diapers. But I won't be home until late."

I clicked END before she had a chance to say anything else.

"Avery?" Brett asked as he plopped himself down on the couch next to me.

My tone of voice must have given me away. Well, and the fact that, if I wasn't on the phone with him, who else besides her would I be talking to at ten p.m. on a Saturday? "Don't get me started. Where have you been, anyway? It's been two hours since I last saw you. Please don't tell me—"

"Adrienne Thorne," we both said in unison.

"She found you then."

"She did. Good news is that I made her understand definitively that we would not take on her project, and then I hooked her up with August. He has that side corp he bought into, and turns out they're looking to sponsor something exactly like what Adrienne is offering."

I clapped my hand over my mouth in dramatic excitement—dramatic because of the gesture, though to tell the truth, it really was exciting to get her off our backs. "Too bad for August Sebastian, but this calls for a celebration!" I lifted up the empty bottle and turned it upside down. "Too bad we're out of bubbles. Don't judge! I spilled."

He nodded to the second bottle. "What about that one?"

"I'm scared to open it."

He held his hand out with a give-it-to-me gesture. "It was definitely time to be done with her. She asked me to dance, and—"

"And you couldn't say no because that's who you are, go on."

He grinned sheepishly. "And she might have gotten a little handsy."

"Grandma Thorne copped a feel of your ass?!" I was laughing so hard, tears came to my eyes.

"Hey. Groping without consent is not funny."

"Well. I mean, it kind of is when it's Adrienne Thorne doing the groping."

He shot me a daggered look as he worked on opening the bottle, but the smile was still there. Then the cork shot out, and I was laughing again at the unexpected pop and the champagne dripping over his hand.

I swallowed the impulse to lick the alcohol off his body and then shook off the swoony wave of my tummy when he pulled out his pocket square to clean himself off before bringing the bottle to his lips to catch the rest of the overflow.

By the time he handed it to me, the champagne had settled, but the butterflies in my stomach were still fluttering.

Damn men in overpriced suits.

"You can hardly blame her," I said, taking the bottle from him.

"You're quite a catch in your three-piece. Is it Armani?" I reached my free hand out to finger the material of his jacket. Or to accidentally brush my knuckles against his taut chest underneath. Same diff.

"I don't remember what I'm wearing. It might be Canali." His eyes pinned to my hand, like he was as fascinated with the possibility of us touching as I was, and for some reason that made my breath catch.

I pulled my eyes and my hand away, but not soon enough to stop goosebumps from sprouting down my arms. "Well. You look good."

"You do too." His voice was soft, and I had to quickly take a sip of champagne before I did something crazy like melt all over him.

"Anyway." He cleared his throat. "Scott. What happened with him?"

He managed to keep from sounding like what he meant was, "What happened with him *this time*?" but that's what I heard all the same.

Ugh.

Usually, I loved to dump on Brett about Scott, but it was getting old, and I was kind of liking the moment we were having before his cousin's name popped into the conversation.

But the interruption was for the best. Before I did something stupid like take advantage of my BFF's attraction to me.

I slumped backward into the couch cushion. "Nothing. Like always. I don't even know why I try anymore."

Actually, I did know why. I wasn't in love with Scott, but I was in love with the way he made me feel about myself. When hot, unattainable, rich-as-sin Scott Sebastian was into me, it was impossible to not feel like I was somebody special. Someone gorgeous and fun and worthy of attention. Someone like Avery.

But then when Scott wasn't into me, I felt like shit, and that was sort of a comfort too. Because that felt more like the truth. I didn't deserve someone like him. I didn't have my shit together. I wasn't gorgeous and fun and worthy of attention, and the reminder was like old socks. I knew how to wear that version of me. It was more real than the dressed up/borrowed from Avery version.

The up and down of it all was beginning to feel like an unnecessary ride, though. "I'm done with him," I declared.

"I've heard that before."

"I mean it this time."

"I've heard that before too."

I glanced over at Brett to see if his expression would tell me how pathetic he thought I was, but what I saw was much more unreadable. "I really, really mean it this time," I said, studying his features for a clue.

"I really, really hope so." His fingers brushed mine as he took the champagne from my hand, and when he brought it to his lips and swallowed, I couldn't help thinking about the fact that my mouth had just been around that bottle, and even though we'd shared a million drinks over the years, it still felt so completely intimate.

What the hell is wrong with me tonight?

I couldn't stop swooning over Brett, which wasn't exactly unusual, but normally I didn't let it get to me so intensely.

It didn't help when he set down the bottle so that he could take his jacket off and give it to me, because God he was such a good guy and he'd noticed me shiver—though the temperature of the night had not been the reason—and how could a man be so completely amazing and unattached?

I wrapped it around me like a cape and tried not to let him see me sniff it for his scent.

Yeah, I know. I was a mess of contradiction. I was blaming it on the champagne. No more for me.

A few beats passed, heavy with some sort of tension that I was sure only I felt but I pretended was shared by both of us.

"So Adrienne wasn't the only reason I was caught up so long with the party," he said eventually. Tentatively. As though he wasn't sure he wanted to bring it up.

Which definitely piqued my interest.

I gave him my tell-me-right-now-why-have-you-been-holding-out-on-me expression.

"I think I might have met someone."

Ouch.

I wasn't sure why that was an ouch or even where it was ouching, so I smiled like nothing was wrong. "You mean, like a girl?"

"Well, I'm not gay, so…"

I rolled my eyes. "I was making sure you weren't telling me about a work-related meeting, bitch. You met a girl. Huh."

"Huh? What's that supposed to mean?"

"I don't know. You just don't usually meet women."

"I meet women all the time."

"You don't usually tell me."

He seemed to consider that. "Huh. I guess I don't."

Over the decade that I'd known him, he'd gone from a raging

playboy to a more selective lover. I knew he wasn't celibate, but lately, he rarely mentioned the women he slept with to me, and it had been years since I'd heard him say he actually *liked* one.

Which was too bad. Because he deserved a woman to make him happy.

If I kept saying it to myself, maybe this unexplainable panic would go away.

"Who is she?" I asked, sure the color was draining from my face. Maybe I needed more champagne after all.

"Didn't get her name."

My breathing resumed. I hadn't even realized I'd been holding it. "Ah, that's too bad. Not meant to be then."

"Not necessarily. I gave her my number. For business reasons, but hey. It means I might see her again. If she calls. Knock on..." He searched for something to knock on, then leaned forward to rap his knuckles on the outdoor coffee table in front of us. "Plastic."

The tightness in my chest returned. I held my hand out in silent request for the champagne. I took a long swig. Wiped my mouth. A breeze blew, and the scent of Brett rose off his jacket and tickled my nose, and it was as intoxicating as the alcohol.

Or I was just sad and pathetic and desperate for something that I secretly wanted but was sure I didn't deserve.

Whatever the reason, it wasn't necessarily one of my finer moments when I cocked my head and gave him my prettiest smile. "Hey, um, want to go to your place?"

Chapter Three

Brett flicked on the light, dropped his keys into the dish in the foyer, then strode into the kitchen ahead of me.

I set my purse down by his keys and then lingered at the door, nervous, which was ridiculous. I'd been to his apartment a thousand times and crashed in his spare bedroom so often that I had a toothbrush in the bathroom. He'd invited me to move in officially on more than one occasion, and I'd always consider it until I remembered that there was no way I could afford half of the nine grand that he paid per month for a luxury location in Koreatown with views of the Hudson.

Sure, he'd said I didn't need to pay that much, but no. It was one thing to take advantage of my sister and her rich husband. It was an entirely different thing to let Brett carry me financially.

And there was the other reason that kept me from adding my name to the lease—I was afraid it would be that much easier to end up tangled in his sheets.

I turned my head to look into his bedroom, clearly visible from the foyer. His door was only slightly ajar, but I could see enough of the bed to know he'd made it this morning, as always. The gray duvet was tucked in with tight military corners, a tie laid out on top, and I could vividly imagine the one he wore tonight had once been laid next to it while he decided which to wear—he'd chosen the better.

It was an ordinary glimpse of a man I knew very well, and though it offered no new knowledge of him, it made my pulse race. I felt like a voyeur, spying on a part of his life that I hadn't been invited into.

I wanted to be invited in.

I wanted to mess up those sheets.

I wanted to be tied up with that tie.

Oh my God, I was terrible. We were best friends, and thinking naughty thoughts about him was super terrible.

Maybe he'll spank me for it…

Yeah, right. Super nice Brett Sebastian was probably not nasty under the covers. It didn't stop me from wanting to find out.

"Are you hungry?" Brett called from the kitchen.

Obviously, I needed to tell him no, call it a night, and walk right past him to the second bedroom beyond.

Somehow I ended up leaning against the counter behind him as he poked around in the fridge.

"There you are," he said, slightly surprised to see me when he turned around. "Hungry?"

I shook my head.

Apparently he wasn't either, because all he removed from the fridge was a bottle of sparkling water before he shut the door and leaned against it, mirroring my stance. He opened the cap and took a swallow then handed it out toward me. "Thirsty?"

I shook my head again.

He recapped the water and put it on the counter beside him. Then he returned his gaze to me. It was heavier than it had ever felt before, a weight that I impulsively wanted to shrug off, but instead I held it, and the longer I held it, the heavier it got. The warmer *I* got. The faster my *heart* got.

"Didn't want to deal with Avery tonight?" His voice was deep and sultry, and I wondered if he meant for it to come out that way or if he was as out-of-control as I was right now.

I wondered why he'd even asked the question, because he knew why I'd asked him to bring me home tonight. The tension between us right now was undeniable, as it often was. The only reason it hadn't gone further before was because one of us—usually me—shut it down before it got to that point.

And now we were intensely staring at each other, daring each other to look away like a game of chicken. It wasn't going to be me. Would it be him?

When I didn't respond to him, he asked a different question. A bolder question. "Is this because of Scott?"

A strange ache pierced through my ribs because yes, partly, but admitting that would end whatever this was before it got started. But also because no, I was not here because of Scott, and the reasons that were not Scott far outweighed the reasons that were. Just, explaining what those reasons were to myself was hard enough, let alone to him.

So instead of answering in words, I pushed off the counter, stepped forward, and kissed him.

He allowed me to, at first. Let me gently wrap my mouth around his bottom lip and kiss it once. Twice.

Then he just as gently—reluctantly—pulled away.

Sort of.

His mouth no longer touched my lips, but his forehead was pressed against mine, and his hands had found their way to my hips. "What are you doing, Eden?"

I splayed my hands over his chest. Worked open the button of his jacket and moved underneath where I could feel his body heat through his shirt and the thump, thump, thump of his heart under my palm. "You can't tell?"

His lips moved forward, and I thought he was going to kiss me this time, but instead, he danced them around mine. His willpower was holding on by a string.

I thought about that—how somewhere inside him, there was a part of his brain throwing up caution signs and how a good friend would try to be strong for him when he couldn't be strong for himself.

I could be strong.

But I didn't want to be a good friend at the moment. "You haven't thought about it?" I asked as I whispered my mouth against his.

"I've thought about it."

I moved my hand down his abdomen and over the front of his pants where a definite bulge was forming.

"How much?" I wanted to hear him say it, but I wanted him to acknowledge that he wanted me for himself. So he'd know this was his choice as much as mine.

He stole a quick kiss, as if he couldn't help himself. Fast as it was, I'd felt his tongue swipe across my lip. "A lot."

My breath picked up at his admission, and the space between my legs felt suddenly drenched. I kissed him again, and this time his tongue was more dominant, sliding in next to mine. Stroking me. Tasting me.

The bulge under my palm grew bigger and more tempting, and when I cupped my hand around it, exploring the definition of his cock, he groaned.

I broke our kiss off in surprise. "Fuck, Brett. This is what you've been hiding all this time?" I'd tried not to think too much about his anatomy over the years, and if I had, I would never have imagined he was sporting a cock this size. Long and thick, not too big, but just on the brink.

At least, that's what I was gathering from the feel of it. "Please, oh please, you have to let me see this monster."

He smiled against my mouth. Kissed me again, deeper, longer. Then groaned again, and it didn't sound like he'd groaned because I was working his cock this time—though I definitely still was—but rather it was the kind of groan that said he was still trying to think with his rational brain, and his rational brain wasn't one hundred percent on board. "Eden, Eden, Eden," he sighed, bringing his forehead back to mine.

"Do you want me to beg?" It was playful, but I would if he wanted me to. I was about to even if he didn't want me to.

He chuckled. "Maybe."

While his head was hesitating, his hands weren't. One had made its way under my dress, and before I could start in on the pleading, his fingers had found my pussy when apparently he'd been expecting something else, because he jerked back, gathered my skirt up so he could see what was underneath, and groaned yet again. "You've been walking around with no panties all night? Fuck, Eden."

It wasn't a good time to mention they'd only been missing since Scott had taken them for a souvenir.

I couldn't have mentioned it anyway because he dragged a finger through my pussy lips and up to my clit, and oh my God, the spark of electricity that surged through me at his touch could have lit up the Empire State Building. I didn't even recognize the sound that escaped my throat.

"You keep it bare for him?" he asked, his voice raw.

He was thinking about Scott anyway, it appeared. That jagged pain in my ribs returned. The last person I wanted Brett to be thinking about right now was his cousin. Scott was the last person I wanted to be thinking about.

But it seemed Brett didn't really care about the answer because he ravished my mouth with his, kissing me greedily as his hand continued to stroke my pussy.

Not to be outdone, I rubbed his cock up and down over his pants with increased pressure. He was so fucking big, and I could swear he was getting even bigger as he ground against my hand, and it scared me and delighted me to think that it was very likely that that huge cock would be inside of me before the night was over.

Scared me and delighted me not because I was worried about his size, but because the idea of Brett being inside of me like that—when he was already inside of me in so many other ways—felt so incredibly Big and Right.

As much as I'd ever chased after other men, I could honestly say at that moment that I had never wanted anything in my life as much as I wanted Brett Sebastian.

All of a sudden, he broke the kiss. His hand came off my pussy and yanked mine off his cock. He held my wrist in the air and met my gaze head on.

"I told you I'll beg," I said before he could say he was putting an end to this. "On my knees if you prefer."

His green eyes went darker, if that was even possible. "Two things we need to get clear: nothing changes our friendship. Losing what we have is not worth however out-of-this-world fucking you will be, and I need you to promise that doesn't change."

"Never. We can handle this without letting it change anything." I believed it as I said it, but I would have said anything for him to keep touching me. "What's the second thing?"

He studied me, as if making sure we were really settled on the first thing before he went on to the second. Finally, he said, "The second thing is that I'm the one in charge."

Before I knew what was happening, he had me flipped around and bent over the counter that had been behind me. My dress was pushed up around my waist, and I could feel his hot gaze on my backside.

"This ass," he said, taking my cheeks into his hands and squeezing, "has taunted me for a decade. No one has a right to look as hot in yoga pants as you do. I can't even tell you how many times I've fisted myself after being dragged to one of your Ashtanga classes."

A sharp thwack across my flesh made me gasp.

Damn. Brett could be nasty after all.

"I should spank you raw for that torture. Would you like that?" He spanked me three times fast, and if my moan wasn't an answer in the affirmative, then surely my pussy gave me away when he kicked my feet apart so that it wasn't just my ass on display but what was between my thighs as well.

I was dripping.

It would have been embarrassing if I wasn't so turned on.

"God, you're gorgeous." It was almost a whisper, like he'd really been saying it for himself, and not for me. It was followed by the sound of his belt coming undone, then a zipper.

I turned my head to look behind me—I was dying to get a look at his monster cock—but a strong hand nudged me forward. When I complied, I was rewarded with a pair of fingers dipped into the pool between my legs.

"Did I make you that wet? Tell me it was me." He traced the rim of my hole before dipping inside again.

"This is all you." I was breathless and finding it difficult to get complete sentences out, but letting him know this felt urgently important. It was probably just dirty talk—incredibly hot dirty talk—but from what he'd said earlier, I couldn't help but feel like Scott might be intruding on his thoughts, and I wasn't interested in a threesome. "I am so turned on right now."

His hand trailed moisture from my pussy up between my ass cheeks, and I stiffened, afraid that Brett was interested in fucking me somewhere other than where his fingers had been, which, okay, I wasn't completely against trying that out, but with a dick that size, my wetness wasn't going to cut it. We were going to need a shit ton of lube.

My worry was short-lived, however, when I felt the length of him slide between my ass cheeks, avoiding my entry point and giving me skin on skin. "I could get off just like this," he said. An arm snaked around my waist, and he returned to massaging my clit. "My cock sandwiched in your ass. You, writhing beneath me. I could be decorating your backside in minutes."

Goddammit, why did he make that sound so hot? I could probably get off just like this as well—seriously, I was a whimpering mess from his fingers' mad skills—but I was aching for him to be inside me. When I tried to tell him, all I could manage to get out was, "Please."

Fortunately, he either understood what I wanted, or he wanted something different himself because a few seconds later, I was once again spun around, so fast that a strand of my hair flew into my face.

He swept it out of the way, tucking the brown lock behind my ear, and as much as I wanted to check out that cock, his eyes had me pinned in place.

And then it was his mouth, kissing me. Dominating me. Devouring me.

We'd kissed before tonight—not often, but there'd been a few occasions. Nothing serious. Nights where I felt lonely, and he was there to make me feel better.

Kissing Brett had never been like this before.

Those kisses hadn't held any promise of more.

This kiss showed so much more I could hardly breathe. With his tongue and his lips, he showed me just how he meant to fuck me. Showed me how he'd eat me out. Even gave me a glimpse of what it would be like to be loved by him, and I thought I'd die if it ended, and explode if it didn't.

As the one in charge, Brett decided what my fate would be, and just when I thought I couldn't take the overwhelmingness of his kiss anymore, he broke away. Though I'd been close to bursting, I was like a magnet, and my mouth reached for his again, but then his hands were around me, and he was lifting my ass up to sit on the counter.

His eyes twinkled as he bent one leg and set the heel of my shoe on the counter next to me then the other, and for the first time I understood how much he really *had* thought about this—about us—because I could read all over his face that he'd definitely thought about seeing me like this, thought about spreading me out in front of him.

"Oh yeah," he said, then bent down and swiped his tongue up my seam. "You taste amazing," he said before licking me again.

Then he slapped me hard across my pussy, as if punishing me for tasting so good.

An intense shiver ran through me, and I fell backwards, catching myself on my elbows. "Whoa."

"I know, Edie," he said, following the slap up with another lick, even though he couldn't possibly know. He couldn't. He was still able to hold himself upright. He still had the ability to say more than one syllable words. He could move his tongue and think about where his fingers should be (inside me) at the same time. There was no way he had any clue what I was feeling.

I didn't even know what I was feeling.

I felt upside down. Or turned on high. Like all my life I'd been living on one battery and half the charge, and suddenly someone had put a second one in me, and everything was brighter and more intense. Even the longtime nickname Brett had for me hit me in a way it never had before. Like it was loaded when before it had been one-dimensional. Like if he said it again, it could blow up everything I thought was real between the two of us, and make it so much more.

When he moved to my clit, to suck it and worship it the way he'd promised my mouth that he would, his fingers rubbed some spot I hadn't known existed inside me, and I came instantly. He held on to my thighs as I shook and cried out, forbidding me from moving away from his attack until I was all the way through the climax.

I could still see remnants of stars in front of my eyes when he stood up straight, pulled my face toward his. "Did I tell you you could come all over my tongue like that?" He kissed me, letting me taste myself.

"I don't think you gave me much of a choice." Oh, hey. I'd recovered the ability to make words again.

"That's right, I didn't." He brought his hand to wrap around the front of my neck, and the two fingers that had been inside me passed my lips. I sucked him clean without him asking me to. "My cock is so fucking hard."

I'd just come, and I felt hard too.

Or whatever the female equivalent was. I was desperate with need, that's what I was.

I was also desperate to finally meet this cock of his face to face. I reached down between us, and when my hand closed around his erection, he pulled his head back so that he could watch.

Which meant that I could watch.

And holy mother of monsters, his cock was stunning. "I have no words," I stammered. "I mean, I have a whole string of words, and none of them are words I would have thought appropriate for a penis."

He smiled and tried to kiss me, but I dodged his lips, too enamored with the heavy flesh in my hand. I stroked him up and down, admiring the velvety softness of his head and the rigid bump of veins down his shaft. "This is seriously a gorgeous cock, Brett. I'm...I'm..." Proud? Amazed? Happy? All of the above, but what I landed on was, "So lucky."

He laughed through a growl, most likely brought on by the change in my grasp around him. I looked up at his face, awed by his heavy-lidded expression, and when I returned my gaze to his beautiful giant, I realized he'd taken a step toward me or I'd scooted more toward the edge of the counter, because now he was right there, only an inch away from my opening.

His cock jerked in my hand.

My pussy throbbed.

"I really want you to put that inside me," I whispered.

He moved forward, sliding the length of his cock against my wet seam the way he had between my ass cheeks. "Do you?"

"Yes." I couldn't take my eyes off him, how big he looked as he slid against my pussy. It felt thrilling, having him so close to where my need ached, and torturous all at the same time. "Please, yes."

This time when he slid down my seam, his head notched at my hole. His cock pulsed against me. "The condoms are in my bedroom."

Which meant we'd go to the bedroom.

But I didn't move at all, and the only move he made was to nudge his cock inside me—just the tip. We moaned in unison, our foreheads pinned together as we watched the erotic sight between us.

"Oh my God, you're going to feel so good," I panted.

"You're going to fucking kill me, Edie." He pulled out, only to shove in again—just the tip.

"This is so bad." So very bad. Like playing Russian Roulette. Hoping we had the strength to pull ourselves apart before having unprotected sex in his kitchen. Yeah, I was on birth control, but neither of us were celibate, and there were other things to worry about besides unwanted babies.

"Potentially very, very bad," he said in response, and when I moved my eyes toward him, I realized he was watching me now instead of his cock, and I had a very sure feeling that he wasn't talking about us not having a condom.

But I didn't want to think about what he really meant.

I didn't want to give myself a chance to think he might be right.

I definitely didn't want him to think long enough to decide we needed to stop.

So I tilted his chin up so that his lips were a whisper away from mine and did what I'd been threatening to do—I begged. "Please, please, please, Brett, take me to your bedroom and fuck me with that monster cock right now."

Then he took me to his bedroom, and it was hours before either of us were thinking anything again.

Chapter Four

The smell of bacon pulled me from my sleep with a reminder that I was not at home. Avery didn't believe in eating anything with more than twenty percent fat (in other words, anything that tasted good), so her Sunday breakfast consisted of egg whites and turkey, neither of which filled the air with a delicious fragrance.

That meant I'd spent the night at Brett's.

As soon as I rolled over, muscles I hadn't remembered having screamed out in resistance.

And then I remembered what else I'd done last night.

With Brett.

Over and over.

Flashes of our sexcapade shot in my head like an advertisement for *Girls Gone Wild*. Man, Brett had skills. That thing he'd done with his tongue…And had I really been bent in half like that? I hadn't realized I was that flexible.

I threw my legs off the side of the bed, and a spasm ran up my hamstring. Ah, I *wasn't* that flexible. I'd ignored my physical boundaries and was paying for it in spades now.

Worth it.

I could barely stand up straight, the very definition of best sex of my life, and I was pretty sure I couldn't wipe the ear-to-ear grin off my face if someone paid me.

I automatically reached for my phone—when you had sex this good, you had to tell someone—and then remembered I hadn't plugged it in last night.

Except, there it was. Sitting in the charging dock on the nightstand as if that was where it belonged. Admittedly, my pink case looked good there next to Brett's graphite iPhone and his gold cufflinks and his Apple watch and *ohmyGodIsleptwithBrettlastnight.*

It hit me now. Really hit me.

I'd slept with Brett Sebastian.

Certified nice guy.

My best friend.

King of cunnilingus—a fact I hadn't known twelve hours before, and now that I knew I couldn't ever unknow. I didn't *want* to unknow. I wanted to be the recipient of his talent forever and ever, amen, and that was why I was about to have a major freak-out.

Only I didn't really feel on the edge of a freak-out. Just that I should be. In fact, I felt really good. Better than I had in a long time, and not just freshly-fucked kind of good, but emotionally and mentally kind of good. A déjà vu kind of good. That kind of good that said you're in the right place at the right time.

I never felt that way after a night with Scott.

Maybe because I'd had higher expectations when I was with him.

Or because he never let me sleep over.

Or because he'd never paused to talk for an hour before a second round.

Or because he'd never even gone for a second round.

But all of those excuses felt too simple.

Though really it was simple, and I was making it complicated. I felt good because it had been Brett. Because I already loved Brett, and I knew he already loved me. I hadn't had to keep my guard up. I trusted him with my vulnerability, and he'd proven he deserved that trust last night as well as on a thousand occasions before that.

So...what did that mean happened now?

I needed some friendly advice, pronto.

Phone in hand, I ran to the bathroom—naked because my extra clothes were in the guest closet, and I had zero idea where the clothes I'd worn last night had ended up—and locked myself in. With my back leaning on the door, I unlocked my screen and pulled up my phone before realizing that the person I would normally call in this situation was the same person I needed to talk about.

Fuck.

Was this why everyone said you shouldn't sleep with your best friend? That really needed to be made clear in the Universal Guide to Life that I frequently wished existed.

Brett wasn't my *only* friend, thank God, but a quick mental analysis of who would both be trusted with the information of my tryst and who might give me solid advice left me with an empty list.

That left my sister.

Goddammit. I'd forgotten the diapers.

So I couldn't call my sister.

But I could call Nolan.

"I got the diapers," he said in lieu of hello. "If that's why you're calling." He sounded out of breath, and the background noise placed him outside.

"I'm sorry. I completely forgot. Is Avery pissed?"

"Eh, you know Avery. It wasn't as critical as she made it out to be. Finch and I picked some up on the way to the park. I changed him on a bench, and now we're doing our Sunday jog. Aren't we, big guy?" He lowered his voice for the last part, the way he always did when he spoke directly to Finch.

In contrast, Avery's voice went up when she spoke to her baby. The two of them together, cooing at their son, never failed to make me and Brett crack up.

Ah, Brett.

My stomach did a little flip-flop just thinking about him.

"Anyway, you're all good," Nolan said, returning to his normal tone. "Ignore any angry texts from my wife, and enjoy your time with Scott."

It was funny how Scott's name made me want to cringe when less than a day ago I'd let him finger-fuck me at a work party.

Cajoled him into finger-fucking me was more like it.

It was also funny how Nolan assumed I'd spent the night with Scott. Probably because I tended to let him—well, Avery mainly—believe things were going better with Scott than they were.

Time to correct that now. "Actually, I'm not with Scott. I'm with Brett. I spent the night with Brett." Then remembering that I frequently spent innocent nights at Brett's, I clarified. "I spent the night in Brett's bed."

There was a brief pause. "...for the first time?"

"Yes, for the first time. What do you mean for the first time? Have you been under the impression he and I were fooling around?"

"I don't know. It's not that unreasonable. Avery and I have often wondered why you two aren't together. He seems a better match for you than his cousin. The only thing we could think was that maybe you and Brett were lacking chemistry in the bedroom department, but to know that, you'd already have had to...you know."

"Nope. First time was last night." My voice sounded tight. I was strangely irritated that my sister had wondered instead of just asking.

"...and?"

"And…" I cut off when I caught sight of myself in the mirror. I had a hickey on my chest. Several hickeys. When I brought my hand up to touch one of the red marks, I noticed my wrists were red as well.

An image of my hands bound behind my back with Brett's tie while he pounded me from behind flashed before my eyes, and I suddenly felt very warm. "And it was the best fucking sex of my life," I finished.

Another pause. "Are you sure you wouldn't rather be talking to your sister about this?"

"I'm very sure." More sure now that I knew she'd had secret thoughts about which Sebastian I should be banging. "I need some advice, not a lecture."

"Hold on. I need to pull off the jogging trail for this." The phone sounded muffled after that. A handful of seconds later, the phone sounded like it shifted again. "Okay. Hit me. I'm ready. What's your question?"

I suppressed a groan. Wasn't the question obvious? "I slept with Brett," I said again, slowly in case Nolan was having a hard time concentrating, what with being outdoors and all that. "You know. My bff of the last ten years? Your best man at your wedding?"

"Yes, I get that." He sounded equally irritated. "So. Are you planning to do it again?"

"That's what I'm trying to figure out! Should I? I mean, it was good—like I said—but you know, it's more than that. We already have such a great time together. We have common interests. We rarely argue—well, not about anything important, anyway—and I care about him, obviously, and he cares about me."

"Oh, I'm certain he's had a thing for you for years."

"Really?" I rolled my eyes at myself because I already knew that he had, and asking him to expound on that was more desperate than humble, but also I was kind of desperate. Desperate for validation that what I was thinking wasn't completely crazy.

But this was Nolan, my brother-in-law, and we were close. I didn't need to be dodgy. "Okay, I knew he probably did. So do I…? Do we…? What do we do now?"

Nolan laughed, and though I doubted he was trying to be patronizing, I did feel a bit of the Eden-never-knows-what-she's-doing subtext that laced most of my interactions with Avery.

"All right. Thanks for nothing. I'll talk—"

He cut me off. "Sorry, sorry. I didn't mean to be a dick. Look, if you want there to be something more between the two of you, you should talk to him. Be honest. Open up. He's really the only person who can say anything meaningful on the subject."

I wondered for a second if I could call Brett from the safety of the bathroom.

"Talk to him face-to-face," Nolan added, as if he could read my thoughts.

"Fine. Fine." I didn't feel fine. I felt anxious and hopeful, and as uncomfortable as the anxiety was, I was even less used to feeling anything optimistic. "I'll talk to him."

"Good."

"Thank you."

"And good luck," he said before hanging up. "You deserve a guy who'll be good to you."

I wasn't so sure about that.

But after a night with Brett Sebastian, I was sure of one thing—every other man paled in comparison.

Chapter Five

While there were presumed benefits of having a conversation with Brett in my current state of nakedness, it seemed more appropriate that I be dressed.

A quick search through his bathroom laundry basket led me to the T-shirt he'd worn at yoga the day before. I did the sniff check to make sure it wasn't a disgusting choice of attire and found that the only thing it smelled of was Brett's natural manly state.

It was a scent that did surprising things to my lower parts. Had I always been so affected by his pheromones or was this a new thing brought on by the knowledge of how incredibly talented the guy was in bed?

I wanted to blame it on the latter, but there was a part of me that I'd refused to acknowledge for years that screamed it was the former.

Whichever, I slipped the T-shirt on and admired myself in his mirror. Still looked like a girl who'd been fantastically fucked—there was no doing anything with my hair and hickeys—but now I also wore the subtext of *I belong to the guy who owns this shirt.*

Maybe that was a little too obvious, but men in romance books always seemed to like seeing women in their belongings. Generally, the woman didn't stay dressed for long, having been ravished on sight. Might as well try it out in real life.

I considered searching for a pair of shorts to wear underneath—from his drawers, not the basket—but I wondered if maybe that was too invasive, and besides, I was eager to see him. Surprisingly eager. As if it had been days instead of mere hours.

I was nervous too. Surprisingly nervous. And it took a good few deep breaths before I gathered my courage and strolled out to the kitchen. He was at the stove, cooking a batch of bacon. The greasy napkin on the counter suggested he'd already eaten the first batch.

I leaned a hip against the counter I'd leaned on the night before, trying not to let lusty thoughts of what we'd done there take over my agenda. "Morning."

"Hey," he said, throwing me a casual glance followed by a longer look when he realized what I was wearing. "You're wearing my dirty laundry now? Maybe we need to draw lines in this relationship—for your sake, not mine."

Not quite the reaction I'd intended.

I sniffed at it again, and still found nothing distasteful about the scent. "I think you have a strange barometer of what's dirty and what isn't." The double entendre hit me after the words were out of my mouth, and I felt my cheeks heat with Brett's grin. "Anyway, I think I look good in it."

"Well. I can't imagine there's anything you don't look good in." He turned back to his cooking, so I had to assume that he was the one blushing now, even though I'd never seen him blush in ten years.

All right, maybe I fantasized he was blushing was a more accurate statement. Point was he'd reacted as I'd hoped after all. Sort of.

Okay, maybe not at all because his attention was completely on his cooking instead of on ravishing, but that was probably better since we needed to talk.

But how to start?

"I assume you want your usual?" he asked while I was figuring out what I should say. "I'm making this batch extra crispy."

My "usual" referred to the bacon cheese tomato omelette he made for me every time I was over for breakfast. Three whole eggs, not just the egg whites, and topped with crispy bacon bits as well as loaded with them inside.

"Yes, please." I was generally polite, but now the simple words felt charged. I'd used them time and time again over the course of the night— begging for his cock, begging for him to let me release, begging for him to never stop—and now I felt more wanton than well mannered.

I studied him, trying to see if the words had the same impact on him, and...nothing. He remained focused on his task, just like he always was. As though it was a regular old Sunday.

Feeling a little deflated, I circled around to the other side of the counter, climbed up on a stool, and wished I'd brought my phone from the bedroom so I could pretend to be flipping through social media like I normally did when he cooked for me. Instead of swooning over his every move like a crazy girl.

Fortunately—or not, depending on how I looked at it—he didn't seem aware of me at all, let alone what I was doing.

Was he just that good at being "normal" or had last night not meant as much to him as it had to me? The longer he stayed with his back to me, the more I began to think I'd misinterpreted his crush and that crazy good sex was just his default with every woman.

Lucky women.

And also, I now hated every woman he'd ever given a second glance to.

I was still only at the beginning of my shame spiral when he finally turned to serve me a gorgeous-looking omelette covered in crispy bacon just the way I liked it and complete with a parsley garnish.

That much attention to detail had to imply he thought I was special, right?

If the plate of food didn't, his eyes couldn't hide it. There was a crackle when our gazes collided, and the corners of his mouth turned upward like he was fighting a headstrong smile.

"It's four eggs instead of three," he said. "I thought you could use the energy this morning."

...There it was. An acknowledgment of what had happened, and now I was the one losing the battle with my smile.

Hell, I didn't even try. I just grinned like an idiot.

But then all of a sudden, Brett was frowning. He reached out his hand to grab one of mine at the wrist. "Oh, shit. I did this to you?"

I looked down at the red mark. "I seem to remember not protesting."

His expression relaxed somewhat. "No, you didn't protest at all."

Ah ha. So he did remember the begging.

I twisted my hand in his grasp so that our palms faced each other and laced my fingers in his. The way we fit together was natural.

He didn't pull away, and the charge around us amplified and energized. I felt alive from the pulse in the air. If this had always existed between us, how had I resisted it for so long?

"Last night...Brett..." I wasn't scared to tell him how I felt now. Just awkward in how to word it. "I had a really good time."

"Yeah? I did too." His thumb now stroked the outside of my thumb, and holy hell, that simple caress sure made a mess between my thighs.

"Like...a really good time."

"Good."

"Like...maybe we should do that more often."

He chuckled as he removed his hand from mine. Not in a rejection sort of way, but in an I-need-my-hands-to-fix-my-own-plate kind of way. "You mean like a friends with benefits kind of thing?" he asked as he turned back to pour the rest of the egg mixture into the skillet.

"Um, maybe? I was actually thinking more like..." Now the nerves were returning. Talking to his backside both helped and didn't. In some ways, it was easier to be vulnerable without his eyes on me. In other ways, his eyes were the main thing telling me that this connection between us was real.

"More like?"

"You know, we're already so close. We spend all our time together. We know each other's secrets. And we...care about each other. Add in sex and that kind of defines a romantic relationship."

He froze.

At least, it looked like he did.

It was a little hard to tell from where I sat. Maybe he was just waiting for the eggs to cook before he flipped them, but it did seem like his back got straighter and his shoulders tensed, and he held that pose for what felt like hours.

It was probably only a handful of seconds later when he reached to grab the bowl of Gouda he'd shredded earlier and poured it into the skillet. "I thought we said we weren't going to let last night get in the way of our friendship."

"We did." I hadn't been prepared for this sort of response. Honestly, I hadn't prepared myself for any response except banging on the kitchen counter again, and it took a moment to figure out what to say next. "This isn't getting in the way of our friendship, though. This is adding to it."

When he didn't say anything, I said more. "Trying it out anyway. Seeing if it works."

Why wouldn't it work? We already worked. Didn't last night prove we worked?

"I'm listening. I'm just..." He folded the omelette in half. "Thinking."

The fact that there was anything to think about was baffling. And irritating. "You've invited me to live with you before."

"Now you want to live together?"

"No." This was not going well at all. "It just seems if you're offering to share a lease that you're already invested in our relationship long term."

"Of course I'm invested. We're good *friends*."

I ignored the emphasis he placed on the F word. "Really, it's amazing we haven't tried to be a couple before this."

He flipped his eggs over, waited a few long seconds, then slid the meal onto his waiting plate before turning to face me. "You've never said anything about considering us an *Us* before now."

I hadn't.

But neither had he.

I swallowed. "You haven't thought about it?"

When I'd asked the question the night before, his expression had opened up, and I'd seen into this vault of stored emotions. He'd thought about me a lot. He'd wanted me a lot.

But now his face was hard, and the vault was completely closed. "That's just not where I see us going."

"Oh." My eyes pricked.

Fuck. It had been a long time since I'd actually cried over a boy. "Crying" over Scott had really just been code for "I'm going to eat a lot of ice cream and feel sorry for myself."

This rejection felt completely different.

That cliché about the knife through the gut? That was how this felt. Jagged and deep and it was not my fault if Brett got blood all over his hardwood floors.

"Edie…I'm sorry."

The nickname had turned me into an inferno the night before. Now it felt patronizing. *Come on, Edie. Get it together.*

"No, no, no. Don't be sorry. It was just an idea." A fucking lame idea, apparently. Though I couldn't really make sense of that because hadn't he always shown signs that he liked me?

"You're just feeling emotional because of Scott."

"Yes, yes, totally it." It wasn't it at all, but I was happy to cling on to any excuse for the very apparent tears I was blinking back.

"Give it a week, and things will be back to where they were between the two of you."

Was that what this was about? He thought I was rebounding from Scott? "I'm done with him."

"I know."

"For real this time."

"Good! I'm glad." He was glad, but he didn't believe me. It was written all over his...everything.

And that made the tears slow.

Because he wasn't actually rejecting me, and this thing between us wasn't a bad idea—he just didn't believe I meant it.

So now I just needed some time to show him that I did.

Chapter Six

"Have you seen Brett today yet? Has he said anything about the dress?"

I leaned an elbow on my desk and hid my face, as though that could hide me from the woman on the other side of the phone.

But there was no hiding from Avery. She knew by now that I didn't answer my cell phone during work hours, and had taken to calling the main line—which I was responsible for answering—instead.

"If he hasn't complimented you in that dress," she went on, "he's a dick, is all I'm saying. That dress is fire."

This was the problem with borrowing clothes from her. It made it harder to pretend I'd dressed for myself instead of to get Brett's attention.

"God, I wish I'd never told you," I groaned. "Wait. I *didn't* tell you. I wish I'd never told Nolan."

"You should have told me."

No, I should have kept my mouth shut. Telling Nolan had meant that Avery was at the door waiting to greet me when I'd finally made it home on Sunday, and because I hated looking like a total loser in front of my goddess of a sister, I'd had to reframe my rejection into something less rejectiony.

"We're feeling things out," I said, repeating what I'd said then. "Remember? Taking things slow. Don't start making plans for renovating my room yet."

She sighed in a way that made me think she really had been making plans for my departure. "What exactly does feeling things out mean?" As though she hadn't asked every day this week.

It was Friday.

It had been a long week.

I pulled a Post-it note off the pad on my desk and wrote *buy lottery ticket* and underlined it twice. She wanted me gone? Well good luck finding an insta-babysitter when I won the Powerball. "It means we aren't rushing into changing our relationship. If something more happens, it happens."

"Does he even know that you want it to be more? Because if he does, then 'not rushing into changing things' sounds like he's trying to nicely say he's not interested."

She was trying to be helpful. Part of me knew that.

But the bigger part of me was too pissed that she automatically assumed I'd been rejected and even more humiliated that she was right.

"You know what, Avery? I don't need your fucking advice."

"Ah. I see. Instead of scheming how to get one Sebastian who isn't interested into giving you his attention, you're now scheming how to get a different Sebastian who isn't interested into giving you his attention. Same shit, different Sebastian. Got it."

Avery's default mode was bitchy when she got defensive.

Like sister, like sister. "At least I don't have to quietly get my orgasms from a vibrator while my husband falls asleep before the baby for the seventh night straight." Hashtag intimate details I shouldn't know about my family but do because I sleep twelve feet down the hall.

It was low, especially since she'd confessed she'd been feeling down about the lack of sex since the baby was born, but her remark had been low too. Mad and hurt and wanting the last word, I hung up before she could say anything back.

Then, because I didn't feel any better, I picked up the receiver and slammed it into the cradle again.

And then I pasted a fake and overly friendly smile on my face because the glass doors swung open, and a very well put together brunette walked in.

I expected her to cross the lobby to check in with me, but she stood in place for a moment, looking a little lost. Staring hard in my direction. Probably hoping that I could tell her where she should be, but in my fragile state, her stare felt hateful, and I had to try very hard not to crawl under my desk with the Oreos that I secretly kept in the back of my bottom drawer.

"How may I help you?" I asked when she finally crossed over to me because I wasn't going to scream at her from several yards away, no matter how lost she looked.

"Yes, I have an appointment with Scott Sebastian." The maliciousness I'd thought I'd seen must have been imagined. Now all I sensed was friendly professionalism with maybe a trace of nervousness. "Tess Turani with Conscience Connect. Ten a.m."

I pulled up Scott's calendar, realizing this was the first time I'd looked at it all day. In fact, I'd barely looked at it all week. In the past, I would have had each hour memorized, searching for the best times to pop into his office with made-up paperwork to sign or a question that I already knew the answer to.

I really was over him, wasn't I?

I'd spent my energy this week thinking about Brett instead, but pining for him looked a lot different than pining for Scott. I'd tried very hard to act natural around him, like the night we'd spent together and his follow-up rejection hadn't affected me in the least. He needed time to see that I wasn't into Scott anymore, and hard as that was for me to give, time was what he'd get.

My surprising self-discipline had kept me from stalking his calendar. Which was why, when I didn't find Tess Turani on Scott's, I had to do a search for her name to find she was on Brett's.

"Oh, there you are. You're not meeting with Scott; you're booked with Brett." My ribs felt tight. As if there was something lodged in between them. He'd called up earlier to tell me where he'd be for his pitch meeting today, but he hadn't given any indication that it was with a woman.

A young, attractive, big-eyed, beautiful-skinned woman.

Well, hello, Green-Eyed Monster, my old friend.

"He's waiting for you in the meeting room." I somehow managed to not sound like an asshole. "I'll take you back there."

"Ah. Okay. Thanks." She sounded surprised. She'd thought she was meeting with Scott Sebastian, the VP of the department, instead of just an account manager.

But she was meeting with Brett Sebastian—the man who could make a woman come in twenty different ways in one night and know the exact perfect breakfast to make her the morning after. Did she have any clue she was about to enter the realm of a god?

With the polite receptionist attitude I'd been hired to exude, I stood up and moved around to the front of the desk. As soon as my back was to her, though, I scowled. Her expensive shoes clicked on the marble floor behind me, evidence enough that she was following.

At the meeting room, I pushed open the door and ushered her in, careful not to catch Brett's gaze because I wouldn't have been looking for it as Just a Friend.

But when she walked past me and Brett offered her an especially warm greeting—the kind of greeting reserved for people who'd met before in a non-business setting—I couldn't help myself, and I threw a glance in his direction.

And that tight thing between my ribs twisted deeper.

He definitely knew her.

He definitely wanted to know her more.

Leaving the door open—because I was a masochistic asshole—I stepped to the side, out of their sightlines, so I could cling to the wall and listen in. As far as I could tell, neither of them even noticed that their conversation wasn't exactly private, which only made the twisting worse.

Who the fuck was this chick?

It didn't take long to figure out that she'd been the woman Brett had met on Saturday night. The one he'd told me about minutes before I decided that I should finally jump the guy's bones. The one he'd said he wanted to see again.

Was she who he'd been thinking about the whole time he'd been with me? When he'd fisted my brown hair in his hand, had he pictured her darker locks? Had he turned me around as often as he had so that the fantasy was better played out in his head?

I felt like I wanted to throw up.

And cry.

And be a different person than I was. Someone who was worthy of Brett's affections. Someone who hadn't wasted ten years chasing impossible conquests like Scott because she was too scared to discover the possible conquests didn't want her either. Someone who wasn't always told no when she put her feelings on the line.

At the sound of my name said in a way that suggested it had been said a few times, I blinked up to see Matthew in front of me. "What was that?"

"Did Paris email you the write-up for the feature in *Business Trends?*" he asked impatiently.

I pulled my attention away from the dark recesses of my mind and tried to picture my inbox. I'd scanned it earlier but hadn't made it through all my emails. "I think so. Let me forward it to you."

At my desk, I found the email and sent it on then was pulled to find the brochures that had supposedly been delivered from the printer but no one had seen and then to sign the technician order to test the office Wi-Fi before I was able to go back to the meeting room under the guise of making copies in the next room.

Paper in hand that didn't need to be duplicated, I stood again outside the door and listened. "I'm one of the lesser Sebastians," Brett said, a joke that I'd heard him spout on several occasions when people discovered he wasn't from the most famous/powerful line of the Sebastian family tree.

Personally, I hated it, but the self-deprecation seemed to charm people into relaxing. "Not a descendent of Irving. Ida, his sister, was my grandmother. I'm just a cousin. Much less powerful, much less formidable."

I strained my ear listening for her response and heard my name instead, coming from the opposite side of me. "I'm making copies!" I exclaimed too enthusiastically.

Scott—one of the greater Sebastians, according to Brett's joke—gave me a quizzical look. "That's...good. Do you know where Brett is meeting with the rep from Conscience Connect?"

"Oh, yes." I perked up. "Right in there."

This was good. Scott Sebastian always upstaged his cousin.

Not good for Brett, obviously, but he generally seemed to take it in stride. He was probably used to it, having been a "lesser Sebastian" for his whole life, and hopefully it didn't wound him too badly right now to have Scott sweep in and steal Tess Turani's attention. But honestly, I didn't care if it did.

Yeah, I was a shitty friend.

Heartache and rejection could do that to a gal.

I was still standing there when, inevitably, Brett came out of the room not a minute later, closing the door behind him. "Hey," he said.

"I'm making copies," I said, a lot less obviously than when I'd shouted it at Scott. "Meeting go well?"

"Yeah." He seemed unsure. Then more confidently. "Yeah. I think we're finally on track to find a sponsorship that can really help our image."

"That's great. I see Scott seems to be interested." Like I said—a shitty friend.

Brett hardened. "Yeah. It does. I'm glad, for Tess's sake."

"*Tess*. You're on a first-name basis with her already." My vow to keep it cool around him was very close to breaking. Usually, Brett was ultra-professional, always using last names with all outside business associates, even internally, and while the Just Friend version of Eden would definitely have pointed out the change in his behavior, it would have come out more teasing than accusing.

"I told you about her," he said stiffly. "Met her at the party."

"You did?" *Not smooth, Eden. Not smooth at all.* "Oh! I think the copier's finished. If you'll excuse me…" I slid into the copy room, shutting the door behind me, to get the papers that I didn't need that had finished printing a while ago since I'd apparently selected five copies.

I bent over and lightly banged my head against the machine. Apparently, I wasn't as skilled at this I-fucked-my-best-friend-last-weekend-and-we're-still-good thing as I wanted to be.

Also apparent was that the tool I'd hoped to use to win Brett—time—was no longer on my side. Not if he planned to pursue a relationship with *Tess*.

For a brief second, I wondered if she'd possibly choose to ignore Brett in hopes of landing Scott. The latter would probably try to bang her. He was known as a playboy for a reason.

But the possibility didn't relieve me for long because I'd had both the Sebastian men, and I knew which one of them was actually the greater—both in bed and out. Only a fool would hold out for the uncatchable Scott when Brett was standing there with an invitation written all over him.

The irony wasn't lost.

I'd been a fool. I knew it. A scared fool. Was I only interested in Brett now because he might possibly be unavailable?

I couldn't think about that too long. I needed to focus my energy on the more important question—how to convince Brett we were perfect for each other. A famous saying suggested that if you wanted something different, you had to do something new.

Unfortunately, I couldn't think of anything new.

So I guess I would just be scheming harder.

Chapter Seven

Scheming to attract someone I knew so well was harder than it should have been. Brett and I had known each other too long. If I made an innuendo, he took it as a joke. If I tried to sound sultry, he asked me what was wrong with my voice. If I bent over seductively in front of him to pick up something I'd "accidentally" dropped, he told me to bend my knees or I'd hurt my back.

Obviously, I still tried.

Saturday, I wore my tightest yoga pants to class.

Sunday, I convinced him to take me for oysters.

Monday, I made him take a love quiz.

Tuesday, I ordered myself flowers and displayed them prominently at the office to make him jealous.

Wednesday, I surprised him with coffee and banana bread from his favorite coffee shop.

Thursday, I fawned over Scott like a teenage girl—again attempting the jealousy angle.

Friday, I cried in the elevator. Not as part of my scheming but because none of the rest had seemed to catch Brett's attention at all.

To make things worse, Tess Turani had been at the office every day to try to help a small committee choose a charity to sponsor, and wouldn't you know it, Brett was the main point person.

Well, besides Scott.

Funny how I barely noticed him these days.

And Brett hadn't noticed that I hadn't noticed Scott even once.

Which was why I hadn't noticed that Scott wasn't attending the

Friday meeting until the lunches came in and there were only four instead of five. "Is Sylvia skipping meals again?" I asked Brett when he came into the conference room early to help me set up.

"Scott said the committee could narrow down the decision without him. Did I forget to copy you on the memo?"

Fortunately, that's when Matt and Paris walked in the door so that Brett didn't see me have to grab a Kleenex to wipe my eyes. Thank God I'd stolen Avery's waterproof mascara.

Because seriously, what the fuck? Forgetting me on a company email? It was like all my attempts to get his attention had done the complete opposite, moving me from the category of Best Friends to Barely Remember She's There. Was he trying to make sure I understood I'd been rejected?

I thought about that during the meeting in between refilling drinks and taking away empty trays. That was it, wasn't it? Brett wasn't an idiot. He'd probably recognized that I was flirting, and because he was the super nice guy that he was, he was trying his hardest not to have to say "not interested" again.

I was the idiot. The headstrong fool who couldn't take no for an answer.

I was already leaning against the wall at the back of the room, and since all eyes were on Tess Turani, no one saw me bump my head against the wall once, twice, three times.

Or I thought no one had seen.

But then Brett looked my way, as if so attuned to me that he felt my frustration. "Okay?" he mouthed.

I didn't know why they called that feeling butterflies. For me, it felt more like horses galloping across my insides. Simply because he'd shared fifteen seconds of his attention with me.

When I remembered that he'd given the previous fifteen minutes of attention to Tess, the galloping came to a dead halt. Never mind that she was the presenter and that was where his focus was supposed to be. I'd rarely kept my focus where it was supposed to be when I'd been into Scott. Not by choice. I couldn't help myself.

I wished that Brett couldn't help himself about me.

But it was what it was.

"Fine," I mouthed in response—what else was I going to say? Then I mimed a yawn because as long as he was looking at me, might as well point out that I didn't think Tess was really all that.

Brett rolled his eyes at me, and then he was gone. His gaze back to her for the rest of the meeting.

Which was fair. It was his job to listen to her, and she was most likely very competent, not that I'd heard a word she'd said. I had a feeling if I really listened to her, I'd quickly agree that she deserved Brett's affection more than I did. And I really didn't need more fuel for my self-doubt.

I glanced at the clock on the wall.

Fuuuuuuuucckk.

There was still another thirty minutes scheduled for this meeting. *Kill me now.*

But suddenly Tess exclaimed, "Fine!" boisterously enough to pull my attention. She swept all of her materials into her briefcase with an energy I couldn't quite place then stood up. "Totally fine."

I narrowed my eyes and listened for clues for context.

Of course, Brett jumped up right on her heels. "You don't have to go right this minute. We still have half the hour left to talk more about it. We can make some recommendations for how to present to Scott. Then make an appointment for later. Or even next week. It doesn't have to be today. His assistant probably isn't even back from her lunch yet."

Brett's eagerness to keep Tess in the room made my chest ache. And it had already been aching. At this rate, I was going to be curled in a ball in the janitor's closet with a pint of Ben and Jerry's Chocolate Therapy before the day was over.

"Thank you for the offer," Tess said with almost as much kindness as when Brett had rejected me nearly two weeks ago now. "But I'm actually fired up from all your enthusiasm. Might as well strike while I'm still hot."

"Okay, then. I wish you luck. We all wish you luck."

This time Brett's deflated tone didn't hurt as much because I was stuck on Tess's parting tone.

I recognized that tone.

That was a nervous tone. That was a nervous energy. A specific kind of nervous. The kind of nervous that a woman felt when she was about to see a guy that she could very possibly get it on with, usually because she had gotten it on with him in the past.

It was the kind of nervous I felt every time I was in the room with Brett ever since The Night.

Who was she off to see? Scott?

Well, well, well. Didn't I say that he'd steal the girl from day one?

Poor Brett.

Except I was feeling too sorry for myself to really commit to that *Poor Brett* and instead was a thousand percent ready to rub it in.

Good guy that Brett was, he not only helped set up, but also generally always stayed to help me clean up. I waited until everyone else had gone, and it was just him and me.

Then I pounced. "She's banging Scott."

"What?" He'd been bent over the table, reaching for a crumpled napkin that Matthew had left behind, and now he shot up straight. "Who is?"

"Tess." I was both exhilarated and devastated that he cared so much. "Tess is."

"You know this for a fact?"

I considered. "Not for fact...but—"

He shook his head and went back to his straightening. "She's not like that. She's a professional. I trust her."

I ignored what that implied about me. "And you trust Scott?"

He thought about it for a moment, his eyes turning toward the closed door as though deliberating going after her. Then shook his head. "There's no reason to be jealous of Tess. She's here to get a corporate sponsorship, not to steal your man."

It took me a second to realize he thought I was jealous because of Scott. "You think—? I'm not—!" God, I was so frustrated, I couldn't get a clear thought out. "I'm not *jealous*." At least not for the reason he thought I was. "I don't care about Scott."

"Uh huh." He moved to straightening the chairs.

I ran around to the other side of the table so I was facing him. "I'm not! And I'm not suggesting that she's not a professional or that she isn't serious about her sponsorship. I'm saying that *despite* the fact that she is, she's into him." For that matter, Scott was pretty professional too. He generally left his philandering to off-hours.

Brett paused again. This time he looked at me—really looked at me. "How do you know that?"

"I just..." No way I was telling him that she was a mirror of my own current emotions for Brett, but thinking about that made me alert to the knowledge that we were alone together. Truly alone. For the first time in days. "A woman knows these things," I said softer. "She had a nervous energy about going to talk to Scott. Alone."

He shrugged. "He's intimidating. He controls the future of her pitch. Of course she was nervous."

"Different kind of nervous. Her eyes got dark."

"She has dark eyes."

"They were darker. And she had that 'Am I wearing cute panties?' look on her face. I could practically smell the pheromones shooting off of her."

He laughed, but he was listening to me. Regarding me. "Say she is into him—"

"She is."

He set his executive notebook down on the table. "And he's into her—"

"What hot girl is Scott not into?" In the past, I would have flinched saying that, but today there was nothing.

Brett didn't say anything, but I could tell he realized it too. "And if both of them are professionals...what might happen between them?"

It stung that he cared.

Unless he cared because he knew I could answer the question from experience.

I pretended it was the latter—it wasn't hard with his eyes burning into me so intensely—and slowly stalked around to his side of the table. "Well, it will start innocently enough. She'll walk into his office with an agenda." I stopped, two chairs away from him. "Then she'll forget it when she gets close enough to shake his hand."

"Stupid ritual," Brett said.

"It is. And they might even forgo it since they've met before, but she'll walk up to him anyway. She won't be able to resist."

As though *he* couldn't resist, Brett took a step closer to me. "Then he'd close the distance? To get a better sniff of her perfume."

I was a connoisseur of fragrances, and in her week at the office, I hadn't detected anything notable coming from Tess.

On the other hand, I was currently wearing Marc Jacobs Perfect Eau de Perfum that I'd picked up recently at Ulta.

My heart skipped.

"He'll say something funny so he can casually lean in to do it, and she'll put her hand on him. 'Oh, Scott.'" I placed my hand on his chest to demonstrate.

He looked down at my hand on his pec. "He'll make a comment about her nail polish. How it matches her lip color."

"And she'll know that what he's really saying is that he's thinking about her mouth wrapped around his cock."

The fortune of having my hand over his heart was that I felt when his pulse picked up. He didn't move away when it did.

In fact, he suddenly seemed somehow closer, and the tension in the room turned up to ten. "Will he know she gets what he's thinking?" Brett's voice was a low rumble.

"She'll know. But she'll feel him out." I swallowed and let my fingers trail down his shirt, over his belt buckle, pausing just above the very obvious swell in his pants to look up at him. Nothing in his face said stop, but I needed to be sure.

I had no doubt when his hand covered mine and moved it down until I could feel the shape of his bulge under my palm.

"Show me," he growled.

Show me what Tess would do to Scott? Or what I *had* done?

Or what I wanted to do to Brett?

They were different questions and therefore slightly different answers. Whether it was a smart idea or not to give him the answer I wanted to give him, I wanted to give it so badly that the choice felt out of my hands.

It was a compulsion.

Opening his pants as fast as I could manage. Working him out of his boxer briefs. Stroking my palm down his length.

Then I was on my knees, and my mouth was on him, and the purr that came from my throat as I moved over him was just as involuntary as any of it.

"Yes, yes," he said, more of an order than an encouragement. "Are you wearing panties? Take them off."

Getting out of them was a task with my mouth busy as it was. Brett helped, placing his hand firmly on the back of my head while I wriggled them off. When I handed them over, I expected him to pocket them, Scott Sebastian style—and he did—but first he brought them to his nose and sniffed.

God bless nasty boys.

"Spread your knees and flip your skirt up. I want to see your cunt." If Brett thought he was still impersonating his cousin, I had news for him—Scott was not this dirty. Not nearly.

Though I wasn't really thinking about Scott.

I was literally and figuratively consumed with Brett—his taste, his scent, his groan when I parted my thighs and lifted my skirt. "You're so wet."

I nodded, and his crown tickled the back of my throat with the movement.

"Show me how wet."

This time I groaned. God that was hot.

Using two fingers, I scooped some of my wetness onto the tips and held them up for him to see.

I swore he was harder the next time my lips glided over his cock.

"Use it on me," he commanded.

Use it to lubricate my hand, he meant. Because I gave a good blow job, but I wasn't a deep throat kind of gal—especially not with a monster like his—and I had been making good use of my palm along with my mouth.

I switched my hand out now, wrapping the wet one around his girth in place of the dry.

"Touch your pussy. Get yourself off, too."

I couldn't tell him that I was already ready to burst, what with my mouth full and all, but he seemed to read the way my body tensed up as soon as I put the heel of my palm to my clit. "Don't let yourself yet, Edie. Wait. Wait for me. Wait until I tell you."

I hadn't realized how much I'd needed to be sure he was there with me and not Tess until I heard my name come out hoarsely from his lips.

Thank you.

Thank you, thank you, thank you.

The knowledge didn't help to put my orgasm on pause. I whimpered around him.

"Almost. Almost," he whispered.

I lifted my eyes, expecting to see his closed and found them wide and intensely darting from my pussy to my mouth to my eyes back to my pussy.

He knew it was me with him. He *saw* me. He *wanted* me.

"You'll swallow."

I nodded even though I wasn't sure if it was a question or instruction.

"Good girl." He petted my hair. And then his cock jerked, and his body stiffened. "Now, Edie."

It took the lightest press of my hand for me to explode. Truthfully, I hadn't probably needed anything other than watching him come—experiencing him come. His hips bucked against my mouth, and his hands held my head in place as I shivered with my own climax, my eyes watering while I tried not to choke on the salty taste of him trickling down my throat.

Once again, thank the Lord for waterproof mascara.

"Are you okay?"

I was pretty sure I'd blacked out momentarily, and it was Brett checking in on me, wiping my mouth with a Kleenex, that brought me back to consciousness.

"Yeah, yeah." I was really okay. A bit sticky, maybe, and a lot shaky, but really, really okay.

"Your knees." They were red with carpet burns, but I barely felt them. "Let me help you up."

I took his hand to stand and frowned at the wet spot I'd left on the carpet. Hopefully it would dry before anyone noticed, but I also hoped that it would be permanently stained so that I could have visual evidence of this incredible moment forever.

"Shit, we didn't even lock the door." Brett's cheeks were flushed, like he'd been running. It was a good look for him, and if I wasn't still so shell-shocked, I would have done a happy dance for being the person to put that look on his face.

My joy was quickly dampened, however, when I realized his expression didn't match his glow. Because the door had been unlocked?

Because he thought this was a mistake?

"That was…"

He trailed off, and I was so afraid that he meant to finish the statement with the M word that I finished it with a word of my own before he could. "Confusing."

His hands dropped to his side. "I was going to say incredibly hot, but I see how confusing is probably more appropriate."

Shit.

"I mean, because…" *Because you said you only wanted to be friends, but then you fucked my face with real passion* was on the tip of my tongue until I realized that I was conflating sex with love. Like I always did.

"No, I get it. Mixed messages. I'm sorry. I'm still not…Here you go." He pulled my panties from his jacket pocket and handed them back to me.

I'd never been so disappointed to not lose a pair of good undies.

And I felt rejected all over again.

And still really confused.

Confused why I was like this. Why I couldn't just appreciate what he wanted to offer. Why I had to make it more. Why I was so desperate to ruin an amazing friendship.

"No, no, no," I said, waving my hand in the air like I could erase the three minutes that had passed since we'd orgasmed together. "Confusing because of the role playing. That was weird to think of you as Scott." I hadn't. "And to see how you'd treat Tess." He'd been thinking of me.

Please let him say he'd been thinking of me.

"Ah. Right." He still seemed tense. "Right," he said again, and I couldn't tell if he was relieved or discouraged, probably only because I wanted him to be discouraged. "That was a little different."

"*Incredibly hot*," I corrected with a wink, as if I could own it if I tried hard enough.

"Yeah, that." He flashed a quick smile. "But probably a bad idea considering…"

That we were at work or that I was a fragile little flower? I did not want the latter confirmed, so I didn't press. "Right. Terrible idea."

"Glad we're on the same page." He studied me for a beat, then picked up his notebook. "Uh, we're good?"

"Oh my God, yes. Of course we're good." I punched him lightly on the arm in an attempt to convey the buddy/buddy thing, even though I was pretty sure I'd never hit him like that before.

I dropped my hand quickly.

"Good." He started to turn.

I was suddenly desperate to keep him, though I had no idea in hell what I wanted from him. All I knew was that I wanted to feel better, and for him to make me feel better, but I didn't know what he could possibly say or do to achieve that unless he knew how to make me be a completely different person than the person I was.

But he was standing there, looking at me, and I had to say something now. "Still on for tomorrow?"

"Actually, I might skip yoga. There's a lot to do to get ready for my mother's birthday party."

It was an excuse. The event was taking place in his apartment's lounge, but the whole thing was being handled by a party planner.

"Of course." I'd practiced smiling through heartbreak with Scott so many times that I knew how to deliver it on cue now.

The "heartbreak" with Scott didn't seem like more than a heartscratch in comparison to this, though.

"I'll see you at her party then." With my head held high, I left the room before he could say I was no longer invited.

Chapter Eight

"Happy Birthday, Laura!" I timidly opened my arms up to hug Brett's mother, but she swooped me into her arms with no hesitation.

"Ah, Eden. It's been a while. I'm happy to see you." The woman was one of the warmest people I knew, a rare find in the Sebastian world. My mother had left me and Avery with my dad when we were little, and I barely remembered her, but the fantasy mother I built up in my mind over the years would have been just like Laura Sebastian.

"I got you something," I said, feeling stupid because what kind of meaningful gift could I give someone with more money in her purse than I'd see in my lifetime? That was why I was mentioning it, actually. An apology. "It's silly, though."

Her eyes lit up. "You know I adore silly. Where is it?"

"I left it on the gift table."

"Should I open it now?"

"No. Definitely no. In fact, open it alone." The thirty-dollar find on Etsy was a pillow that appeared to be floral, but on closer look, the buds were actually penises. Before I worked at SIC, Laura had invited me to DBC, her dirty book club, and I'd discovered a whole other side of her that I wasn't sure her son was even aware of. Unfortunately, her club met in the daytime, and once I had a full-time job, I'd had to stop going.

"Oh. I think I understand."

"You do." We giggled, and I felt a sharp ache, wishing I had an excuse to see her more often.

Though maybe it was best I didn't see her too much. It would only give me another connection with Brett when what I needed was less. After the random sex we'd had at the office the day before, I'd had hard words with myself and decided I needed to put our friendship first and give up on this idea that we might be good together romantically.

Easier said than done.

Being here tonight, with him and his family and closest friends, I kept doubting that decision. I fit in here. This was my place, in his world. Didn't that mean we belonged together?

You do belong together, I reminded myself. *As friends.*

Just friends.

The best way to get over him would probably be to see less of him. Obviously, that wasn't an option since we worked together, and since I'd promised him that we were all cool, I couldn't exactly step back from hanging out together either.

Still, I'd seriously considered canceling tonight.

Now that I was here, I was glad I'd come. But behind my smile, I was struggling. Laura's ever welcoming demeanor wasn't helping, and I tried to subtly end the conversation early. "Well, I won't steal you from those that matter—"

She cut me off. "Don't be ridiculous." She leaned in so she could lower her voice and still be heard. "You're one of the only people I actually like here."

"Didn't Brett invite the other ladies from DBC? Did you give him their contact info?"

"Oh, he invited them, but I warned them all that it would be littered with stuck-up Sebastian prudes and suggested they only come by if they wanted to waste the evening. They decided they're taking me for lunch next week instead."

Ugh. That pain again, the feeling of being left out.

But I said, "Good call," like I didn't have FOMO at all.

She seemed to sense it anyway. "I wish you could be there. Do you think you could call in sick?"

I considered it for half a second before remembering I was trying to move myself away from Brett's family, not toward. "I'm afraid not. It's a busy time right now."

"I get it," she said with a sigh. "Well, sit down with me. We can catch up now."

I went with her reluctantly as she pulled me to the sofa she'd been sitting on before she'd seen me approach. Brett had rented out his building's lounge, a space big enough to accommodate the hundred people who'd been invited while still feeling intimate with seating grouped in conversational style throughout the room.

The sofa that Laura had claimed as hers for the night was grouped with two chairs that were currently occupied by Brett's father, Luke, and a cousin I didn't know very well. The two were deep in their conversation, so it was just me and Laura for the moment.

"So has Michele brought the new baby by lately?" Hopefully, if I asked about Brett's sister, it would keep me from having to talk about myself. "He must be almost one now."

She shook her head. "Nope. I've been talking about myself all night. I'd rather hear about you. Seeing anyone?"

My stomach felt heavy even though I hadn't eaten anything all night. "Ha ha," I said.

"Then you're not seeing anyone? Brett made it sound like you were."

I was instantly curious as to what her son had said about my love life, but equally cautious about prying into a subject I was trying not to care about.

"To be honest—" I took a breath, wondering how I could be somewhat truthful with her. It would feel so good to be able to tell someone. To share at least a tiny morsel of this agony that I was carrying—a little dramatic maybe, but that was me. "I'm trying to get over someone right now."

"Oh, you poor thing. Not a good fit?"

Without meaning to, my eyes crossed the room to Brett talking to Scott, who was wearing a scowl, and his brother Zachary, who nodded along with Brett's words. Did we really not fit together? "He doesn't think so."

"That sucks. But between you and me? Sebastians, in general, really aren't all that."

I turned quickly toward her and blushed when I realized she'd followed my gaze.

Then she added, "Especially that Scott. Trust me. I've known him since he was in diapers."

"You're right." At least she'd assumed I'd been talking about the wrong Sebastian. She might have even heard mention of my trysts with Scott through the family grapevine. I didn't know what Brett said about me, and Scott was pretty discreet about his many dalliances.

Though part of me wished she'd realized who I'd really meant. Wished that she would have corrected me. Wished she would have told me to hang in there, that he'd come around.

She didn't leave me empty, however. Giving me a side hug, she said softly, "Hang in there. You'll find the man for you. Who knows? He might be right under your nose, and you just don't know it yet."

Brett chose that moment to look toward me, and our eyes locked. As much scolding as I'd given to it, my heart flipped at the connection. *Or maybe he's under my nose, and I do know it,* I thought.

But all I said was, "Maybe."

Thankfully, I was rescued from Brett's intense gaze and any more personal talk with Laura when Brett's older brother Tyler called everyone together for a toast. I barely listened, but I raised my flute, and when glasses clinked around the room, I tried hard not to believe it was the sound of something inside of me breaking.

I mingled for the next half hour in a mode I usually reserved for work—outwardly present, internally moping. Whether I was avoiding Brett or he was avoiding me, we didn't communicate at all beyond a few shared glances when he found me looking at him.

God, I was obnoxious. Staring at him incessantly like a lost dog. I hoped I wasn't too obvious, but those hopes were dashed when Scott came to stand beside me during the cake cutting. "What's going on with you and Brett?"

"What do you mean?" Had Brett said something about me to him? I hated how hopeful the thought made me.

"Just that you usually reserve the dazed look for me."

"I'm not looking at Brett with—" I cut myself off before I came off as too defensive. "You're full of yourself."

He gave me that smirk that only a few weeks ago would have had me handing over my panties. "You're over me, aren't you, Waters? We should celebrate. Toast?"

I smacked his shoulder lightly with the back of my hand, but I smiled.

Then immediately dropped it when Brett popped up at my side. "What are we toasting?"

I wished I was invisible.

Or if I had to be realistic, that I was quick with a subject changer.

Thankfully, Scott was fast on his feet. "We're toasting how close we are to sealing this sponsorship deal."

"Ah. I'll raise my glass to that." Brett seemed dubious, which was fair, because Scott was not usually the kind to bring up work at a casual function, and I definitely wasn't the kind.

And I'd been smiling when he'd come over. Brett probably thought that Scott and I had been flirting. So much for making sure Brett knew I was over his cousin, but I supposed that didn't matter now.

Yet, with Brett finally standing next to me, it was hard to remember that I had decided to stop obsessing about him. His presence made me feel itchy in my skin, the way I always felt when I was turned on. Like I wouldn't feel right until I was scratched just right.

But it was more than just feeling aroused.

Brett made my chest feel tight and warm all at once. Those horses galloped in my stomach, but I never felt more anchored in place. I wanted to reach out and touch him, because I liked being connected to him. I liked being his plus one—a label I'd frequently held over the years—not because of how it looked to be with him but because I knew that after whatever event he'd dragged me to was over, he would be the one still by my side. He'd be the one who would laugh at my stories from the night. He'd be the one who convinced me I hadn't stuck out like a sore thumb.

He'd be the one who made me feel like it was okay to just be me.

I was *in love* with him, wasn't I? Really in love with him.

How long had I been ignoring that?

The realization had drawn me from the conversation, but something Scott said brought me barreling back from my thoughts. "What are you talking about?" I asked him.

"About this guy." He pointed to Brett, almost accusatory. "He mentioned earlier he spent the day with Tess. I was asking him for the scoop."

Now I was completely present, jealousy spiking hot and fast in my veins. "Brett spent the day with Tess?"

I knew he liked her. This shouldn't have been a surprise. Of course he'd pursue her. Of course she'd let herself be pursued.

Brett cleared his throat. "Yeah. We, uh—"

I cut him off there. I didn't want to hear him talk about her and him as a "we." I didn't have to listen to this. I couldn't. "You know what? I just remembered I, uh...I have to go."

Blinking away tears, I turned and headed toward the exit, not quickly enough to escape Scott's comment. "That was weird."

Then there was Brett calling after me. "Edie! Wait up!"

I couldn't stop. I couldn't look at him. I kept walking straight ahead, dodging anyone who looked like they wanted to talk, pretending I didn't hear the guy I was crazy about chasing after me.

Hey, I should be happy to be finally chased, shouldn't I?

It was too soon to laugh at myself.

In the hall, I pressed the elevator button. Then pressed it a bunch more times when the doors didn't open up right away.

"Eden!"

Dammit.

There was Brett, heading down the hall toward me.

Hallelujah, the elevator opened then. "Tomorrow!" I shouted out to him as I got in. "I'll call you."

Lies. Tomorrow I wouldn't leave my bed.

The doors closed before he reached me.

Then, I remembered—*fuck*—and I hit the button to open the door. "My purse," I said because he was waiting on the other side. "I left my purse in your apartment."

"...Your purse in my apartment," he finished with me. I'd dropped it off before the party, not wanting to carry it around all night.

Earlier me thought I'd been thinking ahead.

Current me had regrets.

I couldn't get home without it. It was too far to walk, and I didn't have any cash or my phone on me. That was why he'd been chasing after me.

And I'd thought I couldn't feel any worse.

"Just give me your key," I said, but he was already stepping into the elevator.

"I'll ride down with you."

"You shouldn't leave the party."

"I won't be missed. It's fine." He hit the button to his floor, and I wrapped my arms around myself and tried to be invisible.

"What happened?"

I waved my hand in the air, hoping that he got the hint because if I had to say I didn't want to talk about it, I wasn't sure I could get the words out without breaking down.

Either he was in the mood to be persistent or he didn't understand my gesture because he started to say something else, but then, thankfully, the doors opened, and I swiftly exited and rushed toward his apartment. My purse was just inside. All I had to do was walk in, grab it, and head back out. Quick and easy.

It felt like forever before he caught up with me, but when he did, he didn't push me to talk.

Until we were inside. I reached for my purse, but he grabbed it before I did and held it in the air, out of my reach. "Please tell me what happened, Edie."

The softness in his voice...he was going to break me.

I shook my head, an errant tear spilling down my cheek.

"What did Scott do?" he asked more forcefully.

Surprise helped me find my voice. "Scott? You think this is about Scott?"

I watched his chest rise and fall before he spoke. "Isn't it?"

"No, you idiot. This is not about Scott. It's about you. You! Watching you move around in the world, talking, working, going on dates, as though nothing has changed. As though we're the same two people we were two weeks ago. You may be, but I'm definitely not."

"Edie..."

I wasn't in the mood to hear another of his attempts to let me down gently. "Do you know what that's like? Can you imagine for one second? How it feels to have to stand quietly by and pretend everything's the same? That you're not in love with your best friend?"

His response to my impromptu declaration came out sharp. "Can *I* imagine? You're kidding me, right?"

"No! I'm not."

"You've been dealing with this for...what did you say? Two measly weeks? Try ten years, Eden. Try pretending away your love for ten fucking years. Can you imagine what it felt like to watch you throw yourself at one loser after another, comforting you through heartache, touching you like it doesn't mean anything? Can you imagine that?"

In all the time I'd known him, he'd never spoken so harshly.

He'd never said anything so wonderful.

And awful. Because I hadn't been sure, but I'd thought he might like me, and I'd pretended I didn't. I hadn't even given us a chance to talk it out. I'd been such a bitch.

"Wait." I blinked up at him. "Was that why you rejected me? Paybacks?"

"Paybacks?" He looked baffled. Then offended. "No. No."

"So then—"

He dropped my purse to the ground, and then I was pressed against the door, his mouth hovering over mine. "Just...stop talking."

And then he was kissing me. Kissing me like he couldn't breathe without my mouth feeding him oxygen. Kissing me like he would never stop. Kissing me like a man who'd secretly loved me for a decade.

And this time when he carried me to his bedroom, I already knew that nothing would ever be the same.

Chapter Nine

Brett kissed me as he walked me into the bedroom, my legs wrapped around his waist. Instead of taking me directly to his bed, he set me on the ground after we'd crossed the threshold and studied me, like he didn't know what to do with me.

Or maybe he just didn't know what to do with me *first*.

Based on the experience of last time, Brett didn't seem to be one who lacked ideas when it came to fucking. Personally, I didn't care what he did to me, as long as he did something.

Just when I feared he'd changed his mind, that this wasn't a good idea after all (again), he scooped my hair off my shoulders with both hands, then grabbed it tightly in his fists. With a yank, my head fell back, exposing my throat.

I waited for his lips to find my skin there—his teeth to mark me like they had last time—but they never did. Roughly, he used both hands to drag me to the wall. There, he dropped my hair and brought his hands to my throat.

Lightly—then not so lightly—he squeezed.

My breath became shallow, from excitement as well as a constricted airway, and for the first time, I considered that Brett might want to do more than just sexy bad things to me. It was a thought I would never have believed possible before, when I suspected he had a crush, when he was the Nice Boy in my life.

When I hadn't thought about him beyond friendship.

Now, the look in his eyes said that the feelings he'd withheld from me were much more complicated.

He might very well want to hurt me.

Honestly? I didn't blame him.

I placed my palms against the wall behind me, a form of surrender. "Go ahead," I said, my voice tight from his grip. "Whatever you want to do to me, I deserve it."

His jaw twitched, and his eyes blazed, and his fingers pressed in the slightest bit harder at my neck. "Dammit, Edie, I could strangle you just for that."

"For what?"

He shook his head in answer, then relaxing his grip and dropping one hand from my throat, he drew his fingers down my body—over one breast, past my bare stomach, over my pussy. The movement was purposefully light. Controlled rather than tentative. I could barely feel it through the layers of clothing—my crop top, my skirt, my panties—and I was convinced it was meant to drive me mad. I had to concentrate very hard not to buck my hips forward in an attempt to get the pressure I needed.

I was rewarded for the effort when he pushed his hand under the slit in my skirt and stroked me over the crotch of my panties, all the while, his hard gaze never leaving mine.

When I let out a shuddering whimper, he stepped closer to me and tightened his grasp around my neck. His expression seemed to be issuing me a silent dare, I just wasn't quite sure what the dare was. To be silent? To not come? To not be turned on? To not be afraid?

Whatever the dare was, I'd lose. I had no control of myself. The sounds I made came involuntarily, especially when his fingers slipped past the flimsy material covering my pussy and found my bare flesh instead. I was already seconds from coming, the evidence of my arousal soaking his hand as he assaulted my clit with a vengeance.

And yes, I was afraid.

Not of what he would do to me physically, because even if he did want to hurt me, I trusted Brett with my life. He would never hurt me beyond what would feel good. Even if a part of him hated me.

What I was afraid of was what I would let him do to me, if he wanted to. What I would give him, if he asked. What he would break inside me, if he walked away again.

If I wanted to protect my heart, now was the time for me to put a stop to this. Maybe that was his dare—run away now or be owned.

Too late, Brett. "You already own me."

I saw his stoic expression melt for the briefest of seconds before his hand flew from my pussy, and he smacked his palm against the wall with frustration.

Even with the loss of his touch, an orgasm rippled through me, fueled as much by his outburst as from what he'd been doing to me. My knees buckled, my back arched as I cried out, and if it wasn't for his hand still at my throat, I was pretty sure I wouldn't have remained standing.

"Fuck, Eden." Brett pressed his forehead to mine. "I can't resist you like this."

"Then don't." I was still writhing, and the hand that had slammed the wall was already under my shirt, fondling my breast.

"And you show up to my mother's birthday party without a bra…" His tone was angry, and it surprised me when my core clenched in response. The tone carried into his actions when he squeezed my steepled nipple to the point of pain. "Everywhere I went tonight, these stood out for everyone to see. Taunting me."

"I didn't mean to." It really hadn't been purposeful this time. The top I'd chosen had been modest, even though it was slightly cropped and had a low back. I'd only gone without a bra because it was impossible not to. More importantly, I hadn't realized he'd noticed anything beyond my face. I'd caught his stare a few times over the night, but he'd never given an indication he'd been checking me out.

Had this been what the last ten years had been like for him? Always quietly aware of me?

I would have been curled into a ball of regret if I wasn't otherwise occupied with the sweetest torture I'd ever known.

"It doesn't matter if you mean to. You exist. That's all it takes." He twisted my nipple sharply before suddenly letting go of me altogether and taking several steps back.

Automatically, I moved forward, desperate not to be away from him, until he ordered, "Take it off," and I understood he was giving me room to undress.

I reached behind to unzip my top, slowly, distracted by the fact that he was unbuttoning his shirt. He'd dressed simply, choosing a white button-down, open at the neck and rolled up at the sleeves, paired with gray dog tooth trousers. I'd been so focused on trying to get over him that I hadn't properly allowed myself a moment to notice how fucking amazing he looked until now—he looked especially good taking off his clothes, if you asked me—and I didn't want to miss a second of watching him while I removed my own top.

My speed was not to his liking, it seemed. "Stop with the teasing, Eden."

His frustration was palpable, and it was impossible to resist toying with it more. "Or what? You'll spank me?"

In a flash, he undid his belt and came at me, pulling it taut across my throat. "Take everything off. No strip tease. Leave the shoes. Don't be undressed after I am."

The "or else" was in the subtext, and tempted as I was to find out what the "or else" would entail, I thought it might not be the best time to push him.

Besides, he followed up the threat with a greedy kiss, and even with the belt at my neck, his mouth reminded me that he wanted me. That he was desperate for me. That he needed to be inside me.

As soon as he broke the kiss, I took off my shirt, followed by my panties and skirt. By the time I was naked, he had everything off but his shirt, which hung open like curtains to the best show in town—that gorgeous cock, standing straight up while he fisted it.

My mouth got wet watching his hand move up and down. I couldn't take my eyes off it. The way he touched himself was erotic all on its own. The way he touched himself paired with the way he looked like he could devour me whole had me squirming with anticipation.

As much as I wanted to keep watching, my view was abruptly changed when he flipped me around to face the wall. Now I understood why he'd wanted me to leave the shoes. His height generally made him a little too tall for fucking while standing, but with my heels on, he lined up with me perfectly, making it easy for him to shove inside.

Which he did.

I cried out at the sudden intrusion.

Then cried again as he instantly picked up a brutal speed. I placed my hands out on the wall to steady myself, but immediately he ordered me to put them down. As soon as I did, he pulled me by the hair until my back was against his chest, then he wrapped his hand once again around my neck and continued to pummel me from behind.

Needing somewhere to put my hands, I reached back and grabbed his ass, which made my breasts stand out even more. They were already flapping, the sound echoing the slap of his pelvis against my ass, and now it felt like they were on full display despite the fact that Brett was behind me.

Validating the feeling, he reached his free hand around and spanked one of my breasts. Hard. Then spanked it again, moving his hand from my throat to my mouth when I screamed.

"Tell me to stop," he said hoarsely into my ear before biting down on my lobe.

If he was asking for me to safe word out, it wasn't happening. "No."

Appropriately, he took that as permission to slap me again. "I like your breast with my handprint."

I looked down to see one breast with red fingertip marks, and instantly, I was coming so hard, his tempo slowed, and he had to really push to get each stroke all the way inside me.

"You're so beautiful," he muttered, and if I hadn't been able to hear the words, I would have sworn he'd been cursing. "You can't decide if you want me in or out, can you?"

"In," I promised. "I want you inside me."

With a growl, he pulled out of me and let me go, as though just by asking for him, I took the option of the table.

Still shaking from my climax, I fell against the wall. "Please, Brett." I peered over my shoulder and found him at his nightstand, retrieving a condom.

Oh, right. Good idea.

He nodded toward the bed. "You can beg over here."

Without hesitation, I crawled onto the bed and flipped onto my back, wanting to see him. Wanting to kiss him.

Seconds later, he crawled over me, the shirt gone now so that he was completely naked except for a condom.

"Please," I said, as he teased my opening with his cock.

But it was his turn to taunt me. He put his hand up to my mouth, sticking his finger in between my lips. It tasted like me, and that made me want him inside me even more. "Please," I said before nipping at his fingertip.

He searched my face, and I had the feeling of looking at him through a glass wall. I could see him, and he could see me, but there was something still between us. Something tangible that I was desperate to break through.

I cupped his jaw, brushing my palm across his scruff. "Please, Brett. I need to be inside you."

He must have thought I meant it the other way, that I needed him inside of me, because he sat back on his knees and folded my legs back so my feet rested on his shoulders. Then he pushed into me. He applied the same vigor as he had before—faster, actually, now that he wasn't standing. Bent in half like I was, his cock hit deep on each thrust, and despite the addition of latex, I could really feel him. The entire length and width of him, filling me up, bruising my insides.

And yet he still felt so far out of reach.

My legs between us.

His mouth, far away.

That glass wall.

A tear leaked down my cheek, and while I was sure it was a product of the immense pleasure, I didn't discount that it could have come from frustration. It was a sweet kind of agony I was in. Everything I desired, so very nearly in reach.

If only I could…

Brett closed his eyes. I saw when he did, shutting me out. *No*, I wanted to say, *look at me. Be with me.*

But I was overly sensitive and on the verge of another orgasm, and words weren't forming on my tongue. In desperation, I sat up, taking my feet off his shoulders as I did. His eyes flew open, and he watched me curiously as I adjusted our position, climbing on to his lap and wrapping my legs around him.

I could feel him twitch inside me, but he wasn't moving otherwise. I moved my hips, pulling him in deeper before drawing back and repeating the motion. "Please," I said, kissing him tentatively. A question of sorts. *Please, please, please.*

He placed his palm around my throat, as though he needed that hold to feel like he was still in control, then he brought his mouth to mine, kissing me with his eyes open. His tongue slid against mine slowly. Testing.

Then, with a sigh, he let himself feast on me, his mouth speaking to mine in a language that didn't need words. As he kissed me, his hips moved to meet my thrusts, pushing me faster until he took over, holding my waist while he drove up from below, until I was screaming his name.

He didn't hold back even then, hammering into me until he erupted with a jagged groan.

Exhausted, we fell back against the bed.

I closed my eyes, thinking it would only be for a minute. At some point, I woke to the covers being tugged out from underneath me and then being tucked around me.

Then I was aware of Brett, sliding under the sheets at my side.

My body rolled toward him like he was true north. His arms wrapped around me like I was his. Silently, a prayer of sorts ran through my head. *Want me. Keep me. Love me.*

Maybe I said the last out loud, or maybe it was a dream when I heard him whisper, "I already do," before I drifted into deep sleep.

Chapter Ten

I awoke to the smell of coffee. It wasn't quite as alluring as the bacon had been the last time I'd woken in Brett's bed, but I was still smiling when I opened my eyes.

My smile widened when I realized the coffee was already waiting for me in a mug on the nightstand. In my favorite mug, too. It said "Queen of Fucking Everything" with gold crowns. Brett had received it once in a gift exchange at the office, and when he'd tried to pawn it off on me, I'd suggested he keep it at his house for when I slept over.

When I'd also joked that it might scare any one-night stands into thinking he was already taken, he'd agreed.

I hadn't considered then why he might want women to think he was off the market. Had he been essentially waiting for me all this time?

Then why had he rejected me after our first night together?

Not that it mattered now.

I stretched, and the radiance that had prompted the smile spread through my limbs like liquid sunshine running through my veins. I didn't even care how sore my body felt. Every creak of my bones was worth it.

"Was I too hard on you?"

I looked toward the voice and found Brett sitting on the bench by his window, one leg stretched out in front of him as he watched me. He was dressed—unfortunately—in jogging shorts and a pullover, and even though I'd now seen the glory of him naked, I couldn't help ogling the thick muscles of his thighs.

"Should I be worried that you have to think about the answer?"

I blinked, realizing I hadn't responded. "You weren't too hard on me.

Sorry, I got distracted by the view."

He turned to glance out the window behind him, as though that was the view I was talking about. "It's a nice day. Not too hot. I can run outside instead of on the treadmill."

After last night's acrobatics, I wasn't sure he needed more exercise at all. I considered offering an alternative cardio workout, but there was something guarded about the energy between us. That glass wall was back, and as much as I wanted to press against it, I wasn't sure that was the best move.

But maybe I could find a door if I just kept looking. "I could get dressed and join you. I doubt I have shorts here, but I could find something. I'll even let you make fun of my form."

"I uh, prefer the time in my head."

Honestly, I probably couldn't keep up with him anyway.

That was what I should have said, or I should have left it alone entirely and pretended not to be bothered that he didn't want to be with me, but of course that wasn't my style, no matter how much I wished it was. "Because of last night?" I asked, like I was asking to have my heart punched.

He ran his palms down his bare thighs, an action that brought memories flooding from the middle of the night when he'd woken me up with his cock already sheathed, slipping into me from behind. His hand had snaked around me, and he'd stroked my leg then swept up to massage my pussy before another trip down my thigh.

His touch was so arousing, whether he was touching my clit or my knee, and watching his hands give his own legs the same attention did funny things to my insides.

I forced my head from the thoughts when he spoke. "There are some things from last night that bear reflection."

We were in total agreement there. And all the parts that were pushing for a replay in my head had my thighs rubbing together. If he felt anything like I did, why the hell would he want to be alone? "Do you regret it? I swear you weren't too hard on me. I loved all of it."

"I do not regret the sex." Finally, he showed a hint of a grin, but it quickly retreated.

"If not the sex…?"

His eyes were gravely serious. "We said a bunch of things—"

"Things we meant," I interjected, because there was no way I was letting him take back what he'd said. "Don't try to say we didn't."

"I wasn't going to say that."

"Weren't you?"

"No. Not exactly."

"Then you do…" I wasn't brave enough to repeat the word he'd said the night before. "Have feelings for me?"

He cocked his head in a scolding manner. "I think we're past the pretense, don't you?"

Yes, but panic was bubbling up inside me, and I was desperate for validation that this morning wasn't turning into a repeat of last time. If he admitted he loved me, then it couldn't be. There wouldn't be a reason.

Except...

I studied him, realizing what exactly he *had* been meaning to say. Or imply, rather, because even after how close we'd gotten, how honest we'd been, the guy was too nice to say something that might be directly hurtful.

I pulled the sheet up over my breasts, needing to feel less vulnerable. "It's me you don't trust. You don't think *I* meant what I said."

A beat passed where he said nothing, which said all I needed it to.

Okay. Okay. I could work with this. I'd thought it might be this. I moved to my knees, the sheet still wrapped around me. "I did mean it. I *do*. I can't tell you how much I do."

He raised his brows incredulously.

"Why is that so hard to believe? Because of Scott? I'm telling you, that's over. That was nothing." I growled in frustration because I heard myself. I'd mooned over his cousin for as long as I'd worked at SIC, which had been over a year now. "I get how it sounds. But this is different. You're different for me. We already have so much between us."

"Which makes us easy," he said.

"Easy?" Some of it. Right now was anything but easy, but the good parts had been extremely easy. "What's wrong with easy?"

"Nothing is wrong with easy, it's just…"

"It's just...what?"

He brought his outstretched leg in, his body now tense. "Why now, Edie? Why all of a sudden?"

"What do you mean?"

"We've known each other for ten years. You've never given any indication that you had any feelings before now. What happened?"

I was pretty sure I knew what he was insinuating. "It's not just because Scott had pushed me away. He's always pushing me away."

"So then what happened this time?"

"Nothing happened. I just...I don't know." Did there have to be a reason?

"Because of a night of good sex?"

"It was really good sex." It fell flat, and I realized too late it probably wasn't a good time for joking. "I don't know! I figured it out, I guess."

"Because I told you I met someone?"

"Is this about Tess? Is that why you're having doubts about us?" My stomach knotted at the possibility that he really liked her. Liked her enough to end the possibility of anything with me.

But he threw his head back in frustration, which seemed to indicate that was a no, and I had the distinct feeling he wanted to strangle me, and not in the good way he'd strangled me the night before.

Well, there'd been undertones of anger then too. "Are you mad at me for not realizing sooner?" I scooted forward without thinking about it, wanting to be closer to him figuratively, my body trying to achieve it with literal nearness. "I wish I had, Brett. I just didn't. Don't be mad at me."

"I'm not—" He cut himself off and sighed. "I'm not *mad* at you, okay?"

"Okay." But he still was on the other side of the room, and it felt like it wasn't just a glass wall between us now, but also a very large chasm with no bridge.

And I didn't understand that. Because he'd basically said he'd loved me, and I'd basically said I'd loved him. "So what's the but?"

"But I need to think. I need to clear my head and really think."

"About what?" It came out unintentionally sharp, but I was baffled. What was there to think about?

"About us. About if we make sense."

If we make sense.

There was something both promising and piercing about that statement. He hadn't shut the possibility of us down entirely, and that felt monumental.

But the possibility that we might not make sense cut deep. And why was there even a possibility that we didn't? We'd been best friends for ten years. We obviously had amazing chemistry. We had feelings for each other. What the fuck didn't make sense?

Except I knew what might not make sense—me. Chasing after a playboy Sebastian was one thing. Asking a decent, incredible man—the most decent and incredible human I knew—to consider me as a partner was a different thing altogether.

Not that we were talking about marriage here.

But wasn't that what dating was supposed to be about? Brett didn't date, in general. He hadn't had many real girlfriends since I'd known him, and the ones he had been with had been perfectly suited for him. It was obvious he took his choice in girlfriends seriously, as well as the decision to have one in the first place.

And if he had to think about us, it seemed reasonable that he had to think about whether I fit with him like that. Whether or not I was good enough to be given the label of love interest.

It was possible I was overthinking. I did that.

Still, I was desperate enough to make concessions. *We don't have to be anything official. We don't even have to tell anyone. We can take it day-by-day.*

That was pretty much the recipe for most of my relationships. Seemed likely it was all I was good for.

I'd said those words to Brett so many times when I'd cried on his shoulder. *It's all I'm good for.* He'd always refuted it. Cheered me up and cheered me on. Assured me I was worth more than those assholes who made me feel that way. Sometimes he even made me believe it.

Of course, he was worth more than all those assholes combined, including Scott.

And I wasn't going to make him have to explain that to me. He'd hate himself if he had to say out loud that I wasn't worthy of him. It was enough that he was considering me at all.

"Okay," I said, swallowing first so the word would get past the lump in my throat. "How much time do you need?"

"A week maybe. I don't know."

"Okay. Sure." I forced a smile.

"Thank you." His expression was regretful, and I hated making him feel like he owed me something almost as much as I hated that he couldn't just be mine. "I'm going to go on my run now. I have some work I have to do when I get back."

He stood up. The subtext of the lingering look he gave me was clear, and if I was a bigger person, I would have told him that I'd be gone before he came back.

But I wasn't a bigger person. I was a woman that had to be considered. So I made him say it. "I could really use a quiet apartment to get it done."

There was nothing else I could say beyond, "See you tomorrow."

Chapter Eleven

"Well, that was an exciting meeting," Silvia said as we walked out of the conference room the following Thursday.

"Exciting?" It was possible I'd missed something. I'd been in a funk since Sunday when Brett declared he needed "time to think." I'd been present for Tess's entire presentation, but if something exciting had happened, it hadn't penetrated through my brooding.

"Oh, Henry," I realized before Silvia responded. Scott's father had blustered and bullied Tess the whole time, but that wasn't new. He threw a tantrum at least once a month. I waved my hand dismissively.

"But Scott doesn't usually contradict him." She stopped walking, apparently wanting to take her time with the gossip.

I stopped too, not because I really cared, but because it would be rude not to at least pretend like I did. "He didn't contradict him to his face."

"He contradicted him to everyone in the room."

I shrugged.

Okay, bickering about what had happened in the meeting and whether or not it was notable was probably just as rude as if I hadn't stopped to talk about it at all. I wasn't at my best that day.

I hadn't been at my best all week, but the occasions where I had to share space with Brett were the worst. I'd spent the whole hour trying to focus on my tasks, or rather trying not to focus on him, and it had taken so much energy that I was now extremely drained.

Silvia didn't seem to be put off.

She leaned in closer and lowered her voice. "He contradicted his father over a *woman*."

"You think that was about Tess?"

Silvia drew back as if in shock. "Isn't it completely obvious?"

I *had* suspected there was something up with her and Scott. Maybe if I was ever in a good mood again, I'd enjoy that validation.

Right now, though, I didn't have the strength to be enthusiastic so I feigned surprise and gave her my best *do-tell-me-more* expression.

"Scott's a playboy, you know." She seemed then to remember the office rumors and colored slightly. "Yes, you do know." She wasn't ashamed enough to not go on, however. "So it's very intriguing to see him form an attachment. But even more intriguing is the triangle aspect."

"Triangle?" My skin prickled.

She was already leaning in again, ready to tell me more. "Did you see she and Brett were exchanging texts the whole time?"

No.

No, I had not seen that.

Because I'd pointedly not been looking.

"How do you know they were—?"

She cut me off, too excited about giving me a scoop to keep it in. "They both had their phones, and it was all over their faces. Lots of body language in between typing."

I knew Brett liked Tess. But liked her enough to text her during an important meeting?

While it was strange for Scott to show an attachment (and yes, there was a little bit of an ouch about that, even though I was definitely over him), it was stranger still for Brett to ever not be completely professional. Especially at a meeting with Henry Sebastian, the owner of the company and Brett's cousin.

Or was it second cousin? The whole familial thing got complicated to me after a generation or two.

Point was, I wasn't buying it. And not just because I didn't want to.

"Are you sure that he wasn't just giving her advice during her presentation? Henry's his cousin and all."

"Cousin once removed." Oh, that was it. Leave it to Silvia to feel the need to correct me. "And no. Definitely not. The expressions they were exchanging did not say 'business.'"

I still didn't buy it.

Except, I also did.

I'd been learning Brett wasn't exactly the man I'd thought he was. I'd never have thought he'd let a woman give him a BJ at work in a non-private room, and yet that had happened. I'd never thought he would be the kind of guy to declare his love and then run away, and yet that had happened too.

My chest suddenly hurt.

Without excusing myself, I turned back toward the conference room. Brett hadn't walked out yet, and if this was why—if *she* was why he'd needed time—we needed to have words. Why hadn't he admitted it when I'd asked? Was yet another Sebastian gaslighting and stringing me along?

I caught the door as someone else walked through and stopped in the threshold when I saw Brett was already engaged in a conversation. With Tess. Otherwise alone.

My mouth fell open, and then I forced myself to be very, very still so I could make out their conversation from several feet away.

"Tess…" he said, with a weight in her name that wouldn't be there if this was a professional conversation.

She turned to him. "What? He's a player. I got it. I'll try to make sure I don't smile at him again."

"I'm serious here. He's got a reputation for stringing girls along, even when he knows that they're misinterpreting his actions."

Scott.

They were talking about Scott.

Brett was warning her about him. And he'd spent last Saturday with her—a fact he and I had never gotten around to discussing. It was one thing to have a passing interest in her, but anyone with a head would take those facts and extrapolate the same conclusion: He wasn't just interested. He was trying to *win* her.

As Silvia would have said, *Isn't it totally obvious?*

No wonder he had to think about *us*.

Quietly, I stepped back out of the room and shut the door behind me. In the hall, I tried to steady my breathing, hoping it would relieve the ache of each lift and fall of my chest. Familiar refrains repeated in my head:

This is fine.

At least I'm in consideration.

A not completely interested man is kind of my brand.

Sit on the sidelines and take what I could get. That's what I'd done with Scott and countless assholes before him.

The thing was...

The thing was Brett was *not* my usual brand, and a new kind of man deserved a new kind of approach. And if it were some other guy I was pining over, what would Brett tell me to do? Stand up for myself. Refuse to settle.

Propelled by something I couldn't identify, I marched to Brett's office. "Just grabbing something for him," I said to Julie, his assistant, before letting myself in.

Then I faced the door, leaned against the door, and waited.

And waited.

And prayed to God that the reason he hadn't returned yet wasn't because Tess was on her knees in front of him in the conference room.

And I waited some more.

Finally, I heard Julie outside the office. "Eden's still in there."

"Eden?" He pushed through the door, not staying for her to answer, asking me the question instead with his expression.

I didn't give him a chance to wonder. "You made me think it wasn't about Tess."

He raised a confused eyebrow as he pulled the door shut behind him. "What wasn't about Tess?"

"You said you needed time to think, and when I asked if it was about Tess, you didn't answer, but you very explicitly gave me the impression that it wasn't. But then...you and her...you just expect me to wait around while she makes up her mind?"

"Makes up her mind a—"

But I was on a roll. "Because I've always waited around for men in the past? So you thought, 'Oh, sure. Eden will be there whenever.'"

"Hold up. I have never—"

"Were you just going to keep putting me off until you knew for sure if things worked out with her and Scott? And if it did, then...what? Then you come back and say we're all good? So I'm not even supposed to care that I'm your second choice?"

"Are you fucking kidding me? *My* 'second choice'?" It was a roar. A lion roar. Shaking the air and stealing whatever I'd been meaning to say next. "Do you even hear yourself? I'm *your* second choice!"

"What?" The accusation baffled me, but mostly I was confused about his demeanor. I'd seen Brett mad, but I'd rarely seen him so explosive. I had never seen him explode at me.

"Don't be like that. Don't play like I haven't spent the last year comforting you over Scott."

"Sure, but—" I no longer had control of the conversation, and he ran over me this time.

"Before that, who was it? Rufus. And before him, Erik. And before him...the French guy..."

"Michel," I said softly.

"Right! Not even your second choice, am I? Your tenth? Fifteenth?"

Okay. That was a lot of guys over the years. I gave a weak smile. "Am I being slut shamed right now?"

My attempt at humor didn't put a dent in his cloak of anger. "Then you have the nerve to accuse me of making you *my* second choice? For fuck's sake, Edie...I have waited for you and waited and waited. Waited while you let asshole after asshole walk all over you."

"You could have..." Could have what? Told me that I was making a mistake? He'd done that, every time. Told me I was worth more? He'd done that too. Stopped caring about me?

He'd never done that. I'd known he wouldn't, no matter how frustrated he got with me.

...And I was starting to see the point.

"Oh," I said, softly, a squeezing type of pressure building around my chest.

"Exactly. Then you fell for, of all people, Scott."

"I didn't..." But I did. I had. Everything he said. It was all true.

He took a step toward me, but with my shame and his wrath still clearly etched in his features, it was impossible not to shrink back. "Yes, I'm in love with you, Eden, and I guess I can't blame you for returning to the guys who bring you pain, because I kept going back to you. Even though it hurt to listen to your heartache, I swallowed my feelings. I let myself be hurt over and over. You want to know why I really needed time to think if we made sense? Because I already know the answer. And I wanted it to be a different answer, but I know from experience that it won't be."

"No." I couldn't let him say it. "No. No."

"Because even though you're choosing me now, you didn't ever choose me then." His words were softer, which somehow made them punch harder. "And that matters. I've accepted my place as a Lesser Sebastian, but I value myself too much to be someone's second choice. I can't do that to myself. Not even for you."

A tear fell down my cheek. Then another. Then too many to count. For the first time in...ever, he didn't move to comfort me.

And I desperately wanted to comfort him. "Brett…"

But I didn't have any words, let alone the right words. Not just because I had no defense. That wasn't even half of my agony. The source of the bulk of it was much more unpleasant to face. I'd hurt Brett. Deeply. In ways I'd been hurt. Ways I'd never wish on someone I loved.

"I think you need to leave now," he said after a long beat filled only with the sound of my sniffling.

Dismissal jolted me to action. "Brett, I'm so sorry. I didn't know. I didn't realize."

"It doesn't matter anymore. Just…" He gestured toward the door.

I couldn't accept that. It had to still matter. If it didn't matter, we had no chance, and as bad as it was knowing that I'd hurt him, it was a million times worse if I couldn't fix it. "No, it does matter. I should have realized."

I stepped toward him, my arm out, but he moved out of reach before I could touch him. "I can't do this with you anymore, Edie."

There was something final in his posture, in the set of his eyes, in the thickness of his voice.

"What are you saying?" But I already knew. I'd been dismissed enough to know the difference between *I can't do this right now* and *I can't do this ever*.

"I'm saying I need a break."

"A break to think some more?" I clung to a miniscule hope that this wasn't what I thought it was. It wasn't the no I was so used to hearing. It was just the maybe he'd given me before.

He suddenly looked weary. "A break from our friendship, Eden."

I couldn't make an effort to change his mind because Julie buzzed that his four-fifteen was waiting, and I had no choice but to go this time when he ushered me out.

The truth was that even if I'd had the opportunity, it wouldn't have made a difference. I'd never figured out how to keep an ordinary man.

How on earth would I suddenly know how to keep the best man ever?

Chapter Twelve

Avery's voice droned on and on in the background until suddenly it wasn't far away but loud and close to my ear.

"What?" I snapped, looking up from my phone to find her standing over my shoulder.

"Hey, now," she said defensively. "I don't need to be shouted out."

"I'm busy. You're interrupting me."

"You're busy playing Wooduku. I think you can spare five seconds to tell me whether or not I can throw out some of your leftovers. The fridge is getting crowded."

There was more than one dig in there. One about how I chose to spend my Saturday playing games. Another about how I hadn't bothered to throw out my own leftovers. A third about how I'd taken to eating takeout for every meal the past week because I was a lazy slob who was too antisocial to want to eat dinner with the family.

Oh, and a dig about her cleaning up my mess, because of course she was. Because she was good at things like...oh, everything.

"Whatever," I said, going back to my game. If she was subtly looking for my help, she'd have to ask outright.

And I'd still probably say no.

"I don't understand the answer. Can I or can't I?"

"I don't care!" I blared. God, wasn't it obvious I wanted to be left alone?

"Okay, that's it." Avery marched around the couch so she was in front of me. "Look at me, Eden."

I considered not giving her my attention, but I knew her well enough to know whatever bug she had up her ass wouldn't go away until she told me all about it.

With a huff, I lifted my eyes to her. "What now?"

"I don't know, Eden, you tell me. You've been moping around here for the last week or so, making everyone in this apartment miserable. So what's going on?"

Nothing was going on. That was the problem.

The day after Brett had yelled at me and made me cry—reminder that I've a flair for drama, but the statement wasn't untrue—I called in sick to work, hoping a long weekend could act like a reset button for both of us.

Then on Monday, I brought his favorite coffee and some fancy nut bread that I knew he'd go insane over and headed to his office with a peace offering only to be told by Julie that, "Mr. Sebastian has requested no visitors from anyone today. He's helping the other Mr. Sebastian on a project for the sponsorship candidate."

Right. Work was why he was avoiding everyone.

Except Scott really did have Brett putting together a last-minute documentary series to begin filming ASAP. So perhaps the retreat was necessary. I couldn't know for sure since the one text I'd sent him had received a brusque reply. *I need real time off, Eden.*

In other words, not only was our romantic relationship completely off the table, but ten years of friendship was possibly doomed as well, and all I could do was wait and see.

So, yeah. I'd been in a crappy mood.

"I don't want to talk about it," I said, biting my lip.

In her place, I would have taken those words as a sign of dismissal and would have stomped noisily off to brood. But Avery was the perfect one, so instead, she sat down on the coffee table in front of me and brought out her gentle voice. "Is it Scott?"

I shot her an annoyed glare. "I told you I'm done with him."

"Oh, that's right, it's Brett right now." She gave a sympathetic frown, seeming to remember the last status update I'd given her on the matter. "Are things moving too slow?"

I gave a vague head shake. I hadn't admitted things weren't moving at all anymore, and I didn't know if I could bear the humiliation of explaining.

"Don't tell me he turned into an asshole too. He's such a great guy."

Tell me about it.

There must have been some part of me that wanted to talk about it because I found myself giving her a kernel of gossip. "He likes another girl."

"He told you that?"

I nodded.

Then I felt guilty because although he had told me that, he'd also told me he was in love with me, and I wasn't portraying the scene accurately. "He did, but that was before we slept together. And then I saw him with her, and I told him I didn't want to be his second choice."

Avery snorted. "Well, isn't that the pot calling the kettle black."

I wanted to scowl and defend myself and say a whole bunch of things about *how was I supposed to know,* and *it wasn't my fault he'd been such a sucker for me,* and all that bullshit.

I sighed instead. "That's basically what he said. Only he went much more in depth and said a bunch of things I think he's been holding in for a long time and…" I exaggerated my pout so that I wouldn't cry. "I really really hurt him, Avery."

"Oh, honey." She moved from the coffee table to the couch and pulled me toward her.

I leaned my head on her shoulder, and while I didn't feel immediately better, I did feel a little less uncomfortable in my misery. As much as I hated her for everything she did well, I sometimes forgot how much I loved that she was great at encouragement.

She stroked my hair and rested her head on the top of mine. "You understand why he feels like that, don't you?"

I resisted the urge to accuse her of being condescending. Avery had practically been my mother after ours had left, and while I preferred not to fall back into those roles, I knew deep down this was where that was coming from. She was trying to help, and so I let her. "I do now. He feels like he must be second choice because he's been there all along, and I never tried to get with him."

I sat up and turned so I could face her. "But the thing is: I never considered him an option."

She tilted her head, and I could tell she was looking for the nicest way to say whatever she was thinking.

"Just say it. Whatever it is, it can't hurt more than what Brett said." Might as well see how low I could feel.

She didn't hesitate. "I just don't understand how he wasn't an option. You knew he liked you—you've said several times you thought he did, so that can't be the thing that was stopping you. Were you not interested?"

"No, I was interested. Who wouldn't be? But it's like…" I paused to think of the best way to frame it. "It's like the 'pass' list you have with Nolan. You know, the list you guys have where if you ever meet Michael Fassbender, you get to bang him, and it's cool, and if he ever meets Shanina Shaik, he gets to bang her, and it's cool? You both know it's all in fun because even if you met your pass person, you know they'd never actually bang you."

"Uh, sure, Shanina is never banging Nolan, but I'd like to think I'd have a real good chance at Fassbender."

I leveled my stare. "He's married. With a baby."

Avery shrugged. "So am I. We all have our flaws."

"Point is," I went on as though she hadn't interrupted, "they're on another tier. Out of reach."

"How is Brett out of reach?"

"He just is." That she didn't understand was frustrating. "He's rich. Successful. Sexy as fuck. Monster cock."

"I didn't need to hear that. But also, fuck yeah for you!"

A reluctant smile slipped to my lips. "And he's a really good person on top of all that. Guys like him and Nolan deserve the right kind of woman. I'm not the right kind of woman. That's why I always tend to go after the bad boys. The boys who treat me wrong. That's who's meant for me."

"Wait, wait, wait, wait, wait." She pivoted her knees toward me. "There's a lot of bullshit to sort through here, and I'm not sure where to start. Okay, I'll start with this: Are you implying Nolan is also an out of reach kind of guy? Because first of all, I love him, but that man is not perfect, and second of all, he's married to *me*."

"Right. And you're the right kind of woman." I'd never actually told her that to her face, and I instantly felt awkward.

"That's the next part of the bullshit then—what the hell are you talking about? Me, the 'right kind of woman.' What does that even mean?"

"Well—" I couldn't quite meet her eyes. "You're just…you're good at everything. Perfect mother. Perfect wife. Perfect house. It's like everything you touch is gold. It's actually very impressive. And also quite maddening."

"Eden." She stared at me in awe. "I'm speechless. I don't know what to say. No, actually I do—"

"Because you always know what to say," I pointed out.

"No, no, no. I don't. And what you're talking about, all the perfects you listed? That's façade. That's all the stuff I project to the world because I'm so deeply afraid someone will find out what a hot mess I am."

"You are not a—"

"Because I hide it, but I truly am. I'm jealous and bitter and petty. I don't know what I'm doing half the time. My peers were all able to have babies and keep working. I can't manage just the baby without a meltdown at least twice a day. I'm a terrible mom. I'm losing my hair." She tugged at a lock, as if she'd pull and a bunch would fall out. It didn't. "I gained twice what my doctor said I should when I was pregnant, and have only lost a quarter of it. I failed at breastfeeding—I said Finch wouldn't latch on, but it was me who couldn't figure it out. Nolan sleeps on the couch half the time because I throw a fit for no reason and send him out there and then feel lonely and depressed all night but too proud to go after him. The condominium board? I anonymously bullied Cassandra Sanchez on Next Door so she'd step down because I envied the attention she got, and then ran in her place. I secretly order half our meals from a catering place. I ate a whole pint of ice cream last night by myself in my bedroom. And apparently, I make my little sister feel like crap because she believes all the lies I surround myself with. Eden, I am very, very flawed."

My mouth sat open while I processed everything she said. I hadn't been expecting a confession, and honestly, some of it made me mad. She'd let me believe she was a superwoman all this time, not caring how it would affect me?

Then I laughed. "You order our meals from catering? And Nolan doesn't know?"

"No one knows. Except Mrs. Wenchel because they went to the wrong door one time. I order it early enough in the day, while you and Nolan are at work, and then put it in the oven so you think I made it all."

"That's why you're able to keep the kitchen clean while you cook."

"Because I don't mess anything up." She smiled weakly.

When I smiled back, hers grew to a laugh. Then we were both laughing.

Laughing until I punched her arm, and not all that lightly. "Ow!" she yelped, her laughter ending abruptly.

"You made me think you were perfect."

"I didn't *make* you think anything. And anyway, it shouldn't matter whether I am or not. You can't compare yourself to someone else."

"Oh my God, talk about the pot and the kettle."

She giggled. "I told you—I'm a mess."

I had the sudden urge to hug her, so I did. "What is wrong with us?"

"The patriarchy," she said, hugging me back as tightly as I was hugging her. "And no female role model in the house. Really, there's lots of reasons why the cards are stacked against us." She pulled away and gripped my shoulders so I'd be forced to look at her. "But that doesn't mean we don't deserve good things. I deserve Nolan. We're good for each other. And you're good for Brett. He loves you, and if you love him back, you deserve to have him."

I lost the war against my emotions, and my eyes watered. "It means a lot. Hearing you say that. It probably shouldn't, but it does."

"It shouldn't matter what I think, but I'm glad it helps." Her eyes were watering too. "We really need to learn to be happy with ourselves. Without anyone telling us."

"I know. But the confidence of others sure helps." I cleared my throat. "Actually, I think this is a lesson I've been learning for a while. I know it doesn't seem like it right now, but I think the reason I finally let something happen with Brett was because I've been changing, and I do think I deserve him." Saying it out loud felt uncomfortably bold. "Sort of."

Avery pursed her lips. "*Sort of* is not the kind of talk I want to hear, slightly younger than me lady."

"I'm a work in progress, okay?"

"Fine, fine. Just know I think he's the one who should be asking if he deserves you."

I really did love her sometimes.

"I know this conversation is about you," she said after a beat, "but uh, what exactly was the key to getting you on the pathway to self-love? Was it yoga? Please, don't tell me it was the yoga. I am really not bendy."

"It wasn't the yoga," I assured her. "As for what did, I haven't quite figured it out." I had some idea, but Avery wasn't the first person I wanted to tell.

She seemed to understand. "Well, when you do, you should tell him."

...And now we were back to where we started.

"But he won't talk to me." I threw myself back into the couch, extra dramatic like because I was pretty sure she loved my flair despite constantly complaining about it.

"That is depressing." She leaned back as well, a show of support.

"Have you tried?"

"Enough to know he needs space. I'm trying to give it to him."

She nodded. "Personally, I'd ignore that space, but as I've admitted, my ways are flawed. You should probably give him time."

"Yeah."

"But not forever. Figure out how to talk to him fairly soon. It seems he needs to know he's worth fighting for."

She'd confirmed something I recognized intuitively but hadn't been able to articulate. I knew I needed to fight for him, which was partly why the time away from him had given me so much anxiety.

The other part was I just missed him.

"Okay," I said, glad for the clarity. "I don't know how I'll fight for him exactly…"

"Then you need to figure that out too." Clearly, that was the extent of her helpfulness.

"Thanks a lot."

"I already admitted half my secrets. What more do you want from me?"

"Nothing," I said, giving her one more side hug. "You're perfect as is."

Chapter Thirteen

I resisted reaching out to Brett for another week. I did want to respect his wishes, but honestly, the only reason I didn't break down and contact him outside of work was because I hadn't yet figured out how to fight for him.

The only way I made it through the next week was by convincing myself that giving him space *was* fighting for him. The first step, anyway, and other steps were starting to formulate in my mind. Small gestures I could make to prove my feelings. I wasn't fooling myself—it would take time to build his trust. But I was experienced with sticking to relationships, even when they didn't have a promising outcome. Surely, waiting for Brett would be worth the reward.

Still, it was an enormously hard task not to linger after staff meetings, not to stroll down to his office to ask if he wanted to grab lunch, not to text him with laugh-cry emojis when Silvia came in wearing that god-awful floral pantsuit. Not to drop my mat next to his at yoga and get in trouble for whispering to him the whole time.

At least he'd come back to class. Seeing him made me hopeful. And when he accidentally met my eyes across the room and offered a small smile before looking away, I decided it was time to launch into the next level of Project Win Brett for Keeps.

What I needed, though, was a big gesture to kick everything off. The following week, Scott's assistant, Sadie, inadvertently came up with a perfect opportunity.

"What does she want us to do, exactly?" Julie asked after the assistants' staff meeting that Monday.

Strangely enough, I'd actually been paying attention this time. "She wants us to type up our favorite moments with Scott so she can hang them in the break room and make sort of a memory wall. No names. Leave it anonymous."

Julie made a judgey face. "Um, that's dumb."

"Yes. Yes, it is."

Sadie had admitted she'd heard about it at a team building workshop, and that the assignment was originally supposed to be to share memories about everyone in the workplace, but she'd decided to modify it as a tribute to Scott, who was being promoted out of the department. As the originally intended team bonding experiment, the project might not have been half bad.

As it was now set up, it was bullshit for a variety of reasons. First, it was cheesy, and I hated cheese. Second, Scott's job as VP kept him tied up with people in other departments and outside of the company. He didn't intermingle with half of the staff and probably didn't know many of their names. Third, Scott was the last person who needed smoke blown up his ass. Fourth, even if he did, he never set foot in the break room, so he'd never see it.

Fifth, I was absolutely not relating any of my favorite experiences with Scott. Not only were they private, but they were also X-rated. Besides, after Brett, those once cherished memories with Scott had lost their shine.

I was absolutely not participating.

Until I found a way to make it better.

First thing Friday, I approached Sadie and offered to print, frame, and hang the memories that had been typed up. She'd already bought a bunch of generic standard-sized frames and she handed those over and emailed me all the submissions that had been sent to her over the week.

I spent the morning working on it at my desk. Thankfully, it was an easy enough task, and I had all the submissions done by midday, including my own, which I'd placed in nicer, more ornate frames that I'd purchased myself the day before.

I waited until after the break room was cleared from lunch so I'd have the room to myself, and then, with a level, a hammer, and a box of nails borrowed from maintenance, I spent the afternoon arranging the frames artfully on the wall.

When I was done, I stood back and admired my work. I'd done a relatively good job with the composition, only having to move a couple of my nails when something wasn't even (a sixth reason why this project was bullshit—all the holes that would be left in the wall when these memories were finally brought down), but those were barely noticeable. The important thing was that my frames—the ones that contained the memories I'd typed up—stood out, and they did. Anyone who decided to read these would naturally start with mine simply because that's where the eye landed.

I felt good about it.

Mostly.

A little excited.

A lot nervous.

God, I hoped someone actually did read these and that Brett would find out before my additions were taken down.

And that I wasn't in too much trouble over it.

And who was I kidding? Sadie would definitely come look at it before she left for the day, and she'd surely take mine down immediately.

My plan suddenly seemed as stupid as the memory wall for Scott was in the first place, and I was seriously considering taking my frames down when the break door opened behind me.

I turned around, expecting to have to explain myself to Sadie, and instead, saw Brett.

Well, okay. Kismet.

Except that I hadn't wanted to be anywhere around if/when he read them. Fortunately, since we'd been avoiding shared spaces anyway for the last couple of weeks, it wasn't weird for me to immediately gather my things.

"I just finished up," I said without making eye contact, in case he felt the need to leave first.

"No, it's okay. I'm just…" He pointed to the coffee machine, which was a little strange since usually Julie took care of things like that for him, but also he was exactly the kind of guy who would get it himself if she was busy or even offer to get some for her.

But he didn't walk toward the coffee machine. He stood in the center of the room and looked at the display I'd just put up.

"This the Scott's-a-god wall?"

I bit back a laugh and almost choked on it because oh-my-God-Brett-was-making-small-talk-with-me, and I could hardly breathe. But also, I really had to get out of there, so I gave him a quick, "You said it, not me," and then headed toward the door.

I didn't make it out before he exclaimed, "Hold on."

I froze, my hand on the door, too nervous to turn around.

Then after a beat passed and he didn't say anything more, I was too nervous not to turn around. When I did, I found his eyes skimming quickly over one of my memories then jumping to another one.

"These are all about me," he said, and I decided it was awe in his voice, but quite frankly, it might have been confusion.

"Well, not all of them."

He pivoted to look at me. "The ones you wrote."

Even though they were all anonymous, there wasn't any way he wouldn't have guessed the memories I'd typed up were written by me and that they were about him instead of Scott. They were very specific.

The time we planned Nolan and Avery's first anniversary party.

The time he rode the train out to Harlem to pick me up from a date gone bad.

The time he flew me to Portugal for my birthday.

The time we braved the cold and the crowd to see the New Year's ball drop and then ended up back at his apartment watching it on TV before ten.

The time he sat holding my hand in the hospital waiting room when Finch had the cord wrapped twice around his neck and Avery had to have an emergency C-section.

The time he took me to a kennel to cheer me up by petting dogs.

The time he convinced me to sing karaoke with him at the holiday party.

"I couldn't pick one favorite," I said. "And the ones I included barely scratch the surface."

He studied me. "These were supposed to be about—"

"I know," I interrupted. While I hadn't thought it would go down like this, I had been prepared to explain myself. "But, see, he doesn't matter to me. Not really. Not the way you do. He never did, and I know that it doesn't seem like that, but the truth is that you were the one who was always the Greater Sebastian, as far as I was concerned. You were the one I put on the pedestal. You were the one too good for me to try and reach. I didn't deserve you."

He blew out a frustrated sigh. "Eden, I never—"

"I know you didn't. You have never made me feel like I was beneath you. That was me, all on my own. That's the Eden Waters you met ten years ago—low on self-esteem and prone to pairing herself with men who treated her badly because that's what she thought she deserved. And even though I knew you might like me more than a friend, I couldn't ever believe that you could be the man for me because I knew that I could never be the woman for you.

"Except, little by little over the years, that started to change. *You* changed that. You changed *me*. You told me over and over that I was worth something. That I was worth more than I'd ever imagined. And eventually, I guess I started to believe it."

"Because you—"

"Let me finish, okay?"

With reluctance, he closed his mouth and nodded.

I shifted my stuff to my side and cocked my hip. "You wanted to know why now? That's the why now. You convinced me I was worth you. And yes, Tess showing up and you saying you liked her was a motivator, because while this change has happened over years, I think I've been ready to believe you for a while now. Ready to let myself love you. I just needed a little push."

He took a deep breath, looked from me to the wall, then back at me again. "I don't know what to say."

In my dream version of how this would turn out, he would have immediately swept me into his arms and declared we were meant to be and followed it up by bending me over the break room counter. So admittedly, his hesitance was a little disappointing.

But it was also what I'd expected. "You don't need to say anything, Brett. You've said a lot already over the years. It's my turn to convince you what you are to me. You are not my second choice. You are my favorite person in the world, and I know it will take time for you to trust that, and that's okay. It's my turn to wait. I can wait."

Maybe I was trying to convince myself as much as him, but I did honestly mean it. I would wait. However long it took.

And because I did mean it, I resisted the urge to stay, silently begging for some form of encouragement, and forced myself to turn around and leave.

Chapter Fourteen

"I don't care if cheugy is a word used on TikTok. You cannot use it in a Scrabble game."

I agreed with Avery, but her seriousness about the issue had me working hard to suppress a laugh. A quick glance at Nolan said his challenge was mostly meant to wind her up, and it was working.

"I really don't think that's right," he protested. "The rules say the word has to be in the dictionary. Does it specify which dictionary? Urban dictionary should count."

"Urban dictionary should not count!" she practically screamed, her eyes wide, her face red and puffed. Remembering the baby asleep in the next room, she lowered her volume but kept the intensity. "Anyone could make up a word and add it as an entry, and then where would we be? In chaos! That's where."

I gave up on my attempt not to laugh.

Nolan remained straight-faced. "But does it say that in the official rules?"

"Yes!" She typed furiously on her phone.

"She probably doesn't even want to challenge me. She just wanted an opportunity to look up her own word. Now who's the cheater?" He said it to me, but it was obvious he was trying to get a rise.

"*I'm* the cheater? *I'm the cheater?*" Avery jumped from the couch and across the coffee table, almost knocking down the Scrabble board to show her screen to her husband. "Merriam-Webster is the official dictionary of the game. See that? Right there." She quickly typed something new into the phone then turned the screen back to him. "See what comes up when I type in cheugy? 'The word you have entered is not in the dictionary.' Which means you can't play it on the board."

"Oh. Okay. Wait, I didn't mean *cheugy*. I meant *chewy*." He changed the u and the g out for a w. "There. Twenty-six points."

"You can't take your turn after you've been challenged!" Avery went into another tirade about the rules of a challenge.

Nolan finally cracked a smile. "She just gets so serious about it," he said to me. "I can't help myself."

"Why would we play a game if we weren't going to take it seriously?" But then Avery started to laugh as well. "I guess I do get kind of spirited."

I was about to say that *neurotic* was more like it, but the buzzer for the door rang before I got a chance.

"Since you two have descended into hysteria, I guess I'll be the one to answer that." He picked up his empty wine glass, and I suspected he was going to fill it while he was up.

I quickly got control of myself so I could hold up my glass. "Mine too?"

"I'll bring the bottle," he said, already halfway across the room.

"That was fun," Avery sighed, several seconds later. "I needed that."

"Me too." It had been hard saying all the things I'd needed to say to Brett in the break room today. Surprisingly, it had been even harder to walk away. I desperately wanted to text him or call or just show up at his apartment. When Avery had suggested a competitive game of words, I'd scoffed, but then Nolan had opened a bottle of wine, and an hour into the match, I felt a lot better.

Or I did as long as I stayed focused and didn't let myself think about Brett.

Now that we'd quieted down, and Avery was concentrating on her next turn, and Nolan wasn't here to entertain me, my thoughts flew once again to him. What was he thinking? Was he laughing at me? Had I humiliated myself? Had I scared him off permanently?

I lay backward onto the floor with a groan.

"Don't think about him." Avery didn't even look up from her letters.

"Easy enough for you to say." I groaned again.

"Eden's distracting me from finding a bingo," she said to Nolan as he came back into the room.

"That's too bad, sweetheart, but I think the game's over now."

I raised up onto my forearms to give him a questioning look. Sure,

Avery was ahead, but we could catch up. I could, anyway.

"That was Brett at the door," Nolan clarified. "He's on his way up."

Avery actually put down her tiles and looked over at me. "Oh my God!"

My heart sped up instantly, as if I'd been the one to go answer the buzzer and had sprinted the whole time, but I wasn't going to get ahead of myself. "He's here for me?"

"I think that since he specifically said, 'Hey, Nolan, is Edie in tonight?' it's safe to say that yes, he's here for you."

"Oh my God." I jumped up, immediately regretting that I'd changed into sleeper shorts and my *Feminist AF* T-shirt instead of staying in my work clothes. Worse, I hadn't done anything to my face yet, and considering how much I'd been crying from laughter, there was a good chance my makeup was all over the place.

"You look great," Avery said, reading my expression. "Just..." She lifted the edge of her tank and used it to dab at something on my cheek, flashing her tits as she did.

"Stop. I'm not two. And we don't need to see your boobs."

"I don't know. They're good boobs." She continued, of course, and I hoped whatever she'd done had actually helped, because by the time she was finished and her tits were put away, there was a knock on the door.

I grabbed her hands and laced them in mine. "Oh my God."

"He's here."

"He's here!"

"This is good," she said, coaching me through my nerves. "This is really good. You're good. You deserve good things."

"Okay. Okay." Deep breaths.

"I guess I'll get that since you two seem otherwise occupied." Nolan was already halfway to the door. "Come on in. Don't mind the women. They seem to be having a...a...thing. Can I pour you some wine? We're drinking one of Eden's favs so of course it's overly sweet."

"I'm good, thanks."

I dropped Avery's hands and turned toward his voice. Oh, damn. He *was* good. Looking good, anyway. Still wearing his suit pants from the office, but he'd ditched the jacket and the tie. And his shirt was unbuttoned at the collar. And I wanted to peel it down and place a kiss on his skin *right there*.

"Avery," Brett said, nodding a greeting to my sister.

Then his eyes met mine, and the earth moved. "Hi."

He gave me a smile, the kind that felt secret and only mine. "Could we, uh, talk somewhere?"

I moved around the coffee table, coming closer to where he stood. "My bedroom? Or I could change?"

"Your room is fine."

"Okay. Lead the way." I needed the extra seconds walking behind him so I could wipe my sweaty hands on my shorts and exchange one more glance with Avery, who was doing the finger in the hole gesture when I looked over, and my whole face went red just as Brett looked back at me to make sure I was following.

"All good. I'm fine," I said, like an idiot. "Right behind you."

He knew where my room was, of course, having been there a dozen times before, but after several weeks being estranged, his presence in my space felt magnified. And when I closed the door behind us, I felt oddly like a teenager sneaking around behind Avery's back.

He seemed to feel the same. "Are you going to get in trouble for having a boy in your room with the door closed?"

I laughed way too jubilantly, nervous energy getting the best of me. "Yeah, they're…" I didn't have a snappy comeback. "I don't know what's with them. So you, uh, wanted to…hi."

He chuckled. "Hi." His expression fell serious. "Why don't you sit down?"

My stomach tightened. People sat down for bad news, not good news. The last thing I wanted to do was sit down.

But not sitting wasn't going to change whatever he had to say, and defying him wasn't the way to winning him over, so I perched myself on the edge of the bed. "Do you want to sit, too?"

The room wasn't that big and didn't have a lot of furniture, but my vanity had a bench that he could pull over. Or he could sit on the bed with me, which might have been distracting, but I needn't have worried because he shook his head. "No, I think I need to stand."

"Sure, sure." I wrapped my fingers in the bottom of my shirt, hoping that he wouldn't notice I was wringing my hands if they were hidden.

"So. Earlier." He cleared his throat, and every second that he spent not talking felt like an eternity. "I should have said this then, probably. Honestly, I was a bit taken aback."

"I'm sorry. I was trying not to invade your space, but I—"

"Don't." He held a commanding hand toward me. "Don't apologize. Please."

"Okay." My skin was on fire, yet goosebumps were forming all over my arms and legs. Obviously, my body was as confused as my head. If he didn't want an apology, then I hadn't fucked up, right? "So...why are you here?"

"Well, I have more to say, if you let me."

"Sor—" I cut myself off before the apology fully formed. Then I did the zipping mouth gesture and hid the key under my butt before I sat on my hands and tried not to rock back and forth.

"I should have said that the last ten years—me brooding on the sidelines—"

"You weren't really brooding."

He gave me a sharp look, and I immediately slammed my mouth shut. But seriously—how did people stay quiet when they were this nervous?

"That isn't all on you. I could have tried to move things forward a hundred times. I could have brought it up. And I never did."

My mouth opened before I could think about it. This time I shut it before any words escaped, but I was uncontrollably antsy.

Brett's gaze drifted to my bouncing leg and back to my face. "It probably isn't fair to say that you never picked me when I didn't let you know I was a choice."

It was hopeless. I had to ask. "Are you still a choice?"

I was suddenly pushed back onto the bed, his palm over my mouth as he hovered over me. "You just can't help yourself, can you?"

"Not when it comes to you," I said against his palm, and wondered if he could tell I was grinning. Then I put my hands on his hips and pulled them toward mine because he was pinning me down, and that seemed to mean he wanted me.

The stiff baton poking at my thigh confirmed that his body did, at least.

And still he was attempting conversation. He pried one hand off his hip, and then the other, and pulled them over my head. "Don't you want to know why I didn't try to make a move?"

I spread my legs and lifted my pelvis so that I could feel the brush of his cock where I wanted it. "If this is the answer, then yes. Definitely."

"That might be the answer to a follow-up question, if you let me say what I need to say."

I stopped wriggling and gave him my full attention. "Why didn't you make a move on me, Brett?" The truth was I wanted to know, even though I was slightly afraid of the answer. Afraid to find out I'd hurt him in some other way.

He let go of one of my arms and brought his hand down to brush reverently across my cheek. "The only thing I thought would be worse than not having you was losing you."

Emotion swelled through me, and I had to catch my breath. The wall he kept erected between us—that protective barricade of glass—was gone, and for the first time in the ten years since I'd known him, he was completely fragile and soul-bared.

It was frightening being that naked. Being that exposed.

And I was right there with him.

"Then don't lose me," I whispered.

"I'm here, aren't I?" His mouth grazed against mine, and I wet my lips for the kiss I knew was coming, but just as it started, I interrupted.

"This is the answer this time, right?" Once again, I bucked against his cock.

"Yes," he laughed. A frustrated laugh that ended as soon as his mouth met mine.

The kiss began tenderly. Each shift of his lips against mine spoke something new, in a language bodies knew intuitively. Soon, the kiss grew frantic, and our hands raced to tug off clothes—his shirt, then mine. My shorts and panties came off together. His pants were a struggle since he didn't want to let go of me while he stripped. He managed to get them down to his shoes before he let out a frustrated growl and stood up to finish the job.

I giggled, then the sound of Avery and Nolan whispering in the hall made me freeze and listen.

"We're just going to bed now," Nolan called out, and I almost started giggling again. "Good night."

I could hear them shuffle away from us down the hall, then a door shut.

"They think we're having sex," I whispered.

"We *are* having sex." He was naked now. And glorious. And pushing me farther back on the bed so he could settle his whole body over me.

"Not yet, we aren't," I said, but then he pushed inside of me, bare and thick and probing. "Ah," I shivered. "There you are."

"Here I am." He pulled out just a bit before thrusting all the way into me.

My eyes closed briefly while I adjusted to his size. When I opened them again, his were there, waiting for me. Did I really deserve this? Deserve him? "Winning you was supposed to take a long time."

"Are you calling me easy?"

I laughed but then he reached his hand down to my clit, and I shuddered with pleasure. "I'm saying I don't feel like I earned this."

"You never had to earn me. You just had to figure out you were mine."

"I'm yours." I wrapped my legs around his waist. "You're mine too."

"I'm yours."

My lip quivered. He soothed it with his tongue, followed by a greedy kiss. When he tried to pull away to get a condom, I stopped him.

"Don't get it. Be like this with me." Risky, maybe, but he knew I was on birth control, and it hadn't even been two months since Sebastian Industrial sponsored the last corporation-wide, bi-annual STD testing, and we'd both gotten straight As. (Aka, we were clean.)

He didn't argue, and the brisk tempo he assumed said he was ready to not be talking at all, so we kissed instead, and made other sounds. Involuntary gasps and moans of pleasure as his cock moved in and out of me and my pussy clenched around him.

Eventually, the words demanded to be said, not because he didn't already understand, but because they wouldn't remain inside. "I love you."

He slowed, as though he wanted to fully process my claim. I helped him out and said it again.

Then it was both of us, a chorus of I love yous chasing after each other while we raced to climax.

"Does this mean you're my boyfriend now?" I asked when we'd collapsed onto our backs, our breathing still fast. "Except no boy has a cock that big. You're definitely a man." I reached to stroke him. He was still semi-hard, and from experience, I knew it wouldn't take much before he was ready for another round.

Good thing it was the weekend.

"Mm," he moaned. "It means you'll be spending a lot more nights at my place."

"It's like I should move in."

He pulled me closer, rolling me to my side. "You really should."

It was a given now. I'd move in. We'd be official. We'd probably get married. I could picture the ring I'd tell him to get.

...I was getting ahead of myself.

"I'm still going to fight for you," I said, kissing a trail down his chest.

I could feel his heartbeat under my mouth, and I kissed that spot again. "Every day. So you'll always believe that you're the only man for me."

"As long as I get to fight for you, too."

"I guess I can live with that." If fighting for me meant more of his monster cock, I was more than ready for him to bring it on.

I totally deserved it.

Epilogue

I brightened my smile for whichever Sebastian cousin was standing in front of me now—there were too many to remember who was who—then leaned over to whisper to Brett. "Is it bad form to sneak away from your own engagement party?"

His smile didn't drop at all when he whispered back. "But think of all you'd miss: Silvia's catastrophe of a dress."

Oh, this was a game that could make all the small talk tolerable. "Henry Sebastian flirting with the bartender," I whispered at the next opportunity.

It was several minutes before he got a chance to respond. "Avery attempting to become best friends with my mother."

"Adrienne Thorne's obvious attempts to get in your pants."

That one was a winner.

"Excuse me, I need to talk to my bride-to-be for just a moment," he said to the cousin then pulled me a step aside. "For the last time, Adrienne Thorne is not trying to get in my pants."

"You obviously don't know what a woman trying to get in your pants looks like because she most definitely is."

He curled his arm around my waist and pulled me close. "Oh, I don't? Maybe you should show me."

"Once again I ask, is—"

Before I could finish my question, Brett's mother's hand landed at the small of my back, and sure enough, Avery was right behind her. "You two look like you're plotting something," Laura said.

"Of course not, Mom."

"Don't believe him," I said. "He doesn't want you to think bad things about him, but we were just discussing if it was bad form to sneak out of your own engagement party."

Avery's eyes went wide with shock. "Yes, it's bad form! Everyone is here for you. You can't disappear."

"Oh, I don't know if that's true." I scanned the rooftop. "It looks to me like most of the people are here for the free booze and a chance to say they attended a party thrown by the Sebastians."

"A thousand percent true," Laura agreed. "They don't give two figs what you do." I took it as a win that Avery seemed sufficiently shamed. "As to your question, it's not bad form if you take your fiancée with you. Why else do you sneak away at parties if not to get some?" She winked at her son.

Brett's face colored, but it was so slight that only someone who had his features memorized as I did would notice. "I'm going to pretend I didn't hear you say that."

"But we're absolutely going to take your advice," I finished for him. "Bye now!"

He didn't protest as I took his hand and pulled him through the crowd, and after disapproving of the route I'd taken down the middle of the party, he took over the lead, pulling me toward the side where a metal ladder led to a higher level of the roof. It was supposed to be off-limits, so of course when we looked up, a familiar ass was already climbing up after his girlfriend.

"Looks like Scott got there first. Again." He was teasing, though, and not really bothered by it. He'd stopped repeating the Lesser Sebastian joke soon after we officially got together. I liked to think I was responsible, but it probably helped that Brett was given the VP position after Scott left the department. The two were no longer in competition, and their relationship seemed to have improved greatly because of it.

"He can have it," I said. "We have our own spot."

"A much better spot. Should have gone there first." He was already leading me there, but first we had to stop at the bar for champagne.

"I kept a Billecart-Salmon on ice just for you," Denim said, handing over a chilled bottle.

"You know me so well." So well that he didn't bother to try to give me flutes.

"Should I be jealous?" Brett's hand felt possessive on my back side.

"Only if I should be jealous of Adrienne Thorne."

We were stopped three more times before making it to our sanctuary. Once by Brett's sister who had new family pictures we had to ah over in exchange for her oohing over my four-carat diamond—Brett had definitely not gone "lesser" on it, and I hadn't even had to tell him what I wanted.

Then we ran into Julie, who tried very hard not to talk business but still slipped in a reminder or two for my man, as well as a few for me.

Though I still worked at the office, I'd never been into working during off hours like Brett was. I dragged him away when they began to discuss another sponsorship opportunity. The roped-off area meant for the service staff was just in our midst when we were stopped once more.

"Well, Brett. Look at you. First a VP promotion, then a bride. People will start to think you're one of us." Gray eyes under severe brows surveyed me. "Or maybe not."

I'd never met him, but there was no doubt he was a Sebastian. Fuck hot and confident was a very obvious part of his DNA. There was also no doubt that, as far as he was concerned, I didn't measure up.

Brett's hand tightened around my waist. "I'll pretend you meant that as a compliment. But I guarantee you no one will ever confuse me for one of you."

"Mm." He reached his hand out to Brett's, ignoring me now completely. "I suppose congratulations are in order."

Brett didn't extend his out in return. "Nice seeing you, Holt. Next time, don't feel like you have to bother."

Not to be insulted, Holt turned the refused handshake into a clap on Brett's back. "You're never a bother. Remember that when trying to fit in with the Greats gets you in trouble. I'll be here."

Brett didn't respond except to pull me with him. "Let's go, Eden."

"And don't forget a prenup," Holt shouted after us.

But we'd moved on, and now Brett was holding up the rope so I could slip underneath. "Can we not invite him to the wedding?"

"Even better," he said, "let's pretend he doesn't exist."

Any other time, I'd be curious about this Holt Sebastian, but only so I could fantasize about ways that he might die, and tonight was not about the people who tried to make us feel small.

It was about how we were great despite them.

"Do you want to do it?" Brett held out the champagne.

He'd taught me the best techniques, and now I'd become a pro. I took it from him, and soon the bottle was opened with a satisfying pop. "Didn't even spill a drop."

I took a swallow then passed it over to Brett, who had plopped down on the couch. Watching him swallow, I had déjà vu, remembering vividly being with him at this very location, nineteen months before. The night that everything changed. I'd been fighting my feelings for him so thoroughly, I only recognized them in retrospect—how I could never stop looking at him, how my skin tingled in his presence, how I felt like I glowed.

Though that night had started a new course for us, so much *hadn't* changed between us as well. He was still my best friend. Still the person I turned to first on every bad day. Every good day too.

But now he was also the person I got to wake up to and make love with. Now there weren't barriers, and rather than ruining our friendship, adding romance had only made us stronger.

I considered sitting at his side as I had that night but decided instead to hike up my skirt and straddle his lap.

"Hello, there." He offered me the bottle, but I shook my head. I was interested in other things.

"Do you remember much about that night back then?" I didn't have to say which night. We'd attended other parties at this same bar since then, but we'd picked this location for tonight specifically because it had been special.

"I remember all of it. Especially the dirty parts." He ran his hands up my thighs, leaving goosebumps in their wake.

"Did you know when we were here, what would happen when you took me home? What I wanted to do to you?"

"I knew what I wanted to do to you."

"But did you know it would actually happen?"

He thought about it. "I'd imagined it a lot of times, so a part of me always thought it was an option. But yes, there was something different that night. The energy you were putting off—it felt aimed at me in a way that it never had been. I don't think I knew that I was going to get you in bed, exactly—"

"Excuse me, *I* got *you* in bed."

He smiled, otherwise ignoring my interruption. "—but I knew we would be different in the morning. I'd felt myself losing the battle of resisting you for so long. Then, when I had you naked—"

"When *I* had *you* naked."

"—I kept you up all night because I was convinced that was all it would ever be. I had to get my fill. But we must have fallen asleep at some point, because when I woke up, you were in my arms, and it felt so good and right. If you had opened your eyes and looked at me right then, I don't think I would have been able to push you away. I would have had to have you again, and once I had you again, where was the point that I could pull away?"

"So if I'd just woken up earlier, we wouldn't have had to go through those weeks of torment afterward?"

He shrugged. "Would we still have gotten here?"

I ran my hand along the scruff of his jaw and shook my head. "I think I had to learn how to fight for you."

"And I had to learn how to trust you."

"And we both had to figure out we were worth more than we believed."

He took my hand from his face and brought it to his lips and kissed it. Then he looked down at my ring, and I knew him well enough to know what he was thinking. As much as our self-confidence had grown, we were still part of a social structure that had us constantly comparing ourselves to our peers. To our family. The size of my jewel had been determined as much for them as it had been for me.

"Holt...what he said..." He'd pretended it hadn't touched him, but of course it had.

"I don't give a shit about him. Where does he fit in on the family tree?" Obviously he was from the side of the family that had the most money and power, which was not Brett's side.

"He's Reynard's son."

Yep. One of the branches at the top. "Maybe the Greaters should be called the Douches."

He laughed. "There's actually a third category of Sebastians—a sub-genre of the Greaters, if you will. The Brutals. Holt is one of those."

"Eh. I like Douche better." I took my hand from his grasp and brushed his hair off his forehead with gentle strokes. So we had to live in this world with these assholes. It was a constant battle, but we were grounded. We hadn't succumbed to the air of entitlement around us. We knew what was important, and it wasn't the money or the influence. We knew the most important thing was each other, and we'd fight for that every day of our lives.

"You know," I said, "with all these titles you Sebastians have, there's only one that matters, and you're the only one who holds it."

"What's that?" he asked.

"Man for me."

Then we tuned out the party behind us, and I lost another pair of panties to a Sebastian's pocket while we celebrated what all our fighting had won.

* * * *

Also from 1001 Dark Nights and Laurelin Paige, discover Slash, The Open Door, Dirty, Filthy Fix, and Falling Under You.

Discover 1001 Dark Nights Collection Eight

DRAGON REVEALED by Donna Grant
A Dragon Kings Novella

CAPTURED IN INK by Carrie Ann Ryan
A Montgomery Ink: Boulder Novella

SECURING JANE by Susan Stoker
A SEAL of Protection: Legacy Series Novella

WILD WIND by Kristen Ashley
A Chaos Novella

DARE TO TEASE by Carly Phillips
A Dare Nation Novella

VAMPIRE by Rebecca Zanetti
A Dark Protectors/Rebels Novella

MAFIA KING by Rachel Van Dyken
A Mafia Royals Novella

THE GRAVEDIGGER'S SON by Darynda Jones
A Charley Davidson Novella

FINALE by Skye Warren
A North Security Novella

MEMORIES OF YOU by J. Kenner
A Stark Securities Novella

SLAYED BY DARKNESS by Alexandra Ivy
A Guardians of Eternity Novella

TREASURED by Lexi Blake
A Masters and Mercenaries Novella

THE DAREDEVIL by Dylan Allen
A Rivers Wilde Novella

BOND OF DESTINY by Larissa Ione
A Demonica Novella

THE CLOSE-UP by Kennedy Ryan
A Hollywood Renaissance Novella

MORE THAN POSSESS YOU by Shayla Black
A More Than Words Novella

HAUNTED HOUSE by Heather Graham
A Krewe of Hunters Novella

MAN FOR ME by Laurelin Paige
A Man In Charge Novella

THE RHYTHM METHOD by Kylie Scott
A Stage Dive Novella

JONAH BENNETT by Tijan
A Bennett Mafia Novella

CHANGE WITH ME by Kristen Proby
A With Me In Seattle Novella

THE DARKEST DESTINY by Gena Showalter
A Lords of the Underworld Novella

Also from Blue Box Press

THE LAST TIARA by M.J. Rose

THE CROWN OF GILDED BONES by Jennifer L. Armentrout
A Blood and Ash Novel

THE MISSING SISTER by Lucinda Riley

THE END OF FOREVER by Steve Berry and M.J. Rose
A Cassiopeia Vitt Adventure

THE STEAL by C. W. Gortner and M.J. Rose

CHASING SERENITY by Kristen Ashley
A River Rain Novel

A SHADOW IN THE EMBER by Jennifer L. Armentrout
A Flesh and Fire Novel

Discover More Laurelin Paige

Slash: A Slay Series Novella

Camilla Fasbender has a secret.

Underneath her posh accent and designer clothes lies the evidence of her pain.

Every heartbreak, every bad day, every setback has left a scar.

From behind her camera, she shows the world what to see. And it isn't her.

Until *him*.

He sees right through her carefully constructed facade.

And he's going to slash it all to pieces.

* * * *

The Open Door: A Found Duet Novella

I knew JC was trouble the minute I laid eyes on him.

Breaking every rule in my club. I never forget how he made me feel that night. With all the women in that room, all those bodies on display, but his eyes were only on me.

Of course I married him. Now years have passed. Kids have been born. We're still in love as always, and the sex is still fantastic...

And yet, it's also not. Like many who've been married for a while, I long for the high intensity of those days of the past.

I've heard rumors for years about the Open Door. An ultra-exclusive voyeur's paradise. A place to participate in—or watch—any kind of display you can imagine.

My husband's eyes would still be on me. And maybe other eyes too. If that's what we want.

So when an invitation to come play arrives, how could we turn it down?

* * * *

Dirty Filthy Fix: A Fixed Trilogy Novella

I like sex. Kinky sex. The kinkier the better.

Every day, it's all I think about as I serve coffee and hand out business agendas to men who have no idea I'm not the prim, proper girl they think I am.

With a day job as the secretary to one of New York's most powerful men, Hudson Pierce, I have to keep my double life quiet. As long as I do, it's not a problem.

Enter: Nathan Sinclair. Tall, dark and handsome doesn't come close to describing how hot he is. And that's with his clothes on. But after a dirty, filthy rendezvous, I accept that if we ever see each other again, he'll walk right by my desk on his way to see my boss without recognizing me.

Only, that's not what happens. Not the first time I see him after the party. Or the next time. Or the time after that. And as much as I try to stop it, my two worlds are crashing into each other, putting my job and my reputation at risk.

And all I can think about is Nathan Sinclair.

All I can think about is getting just one more dirty, filthy fix.

* * * *

Falling Under You: A Fixed Trilogy Novella

Norma Anders has always prided herself on her intelligence and determination. She climbed out of poverty, put herself through school and is now a chief financial advisor at Pierce Industries. She's certainly a woman who won't be topped. Not in business anyway.

But she's pretty sure she'd like to be topped in the bedroom.

Unfortunately most men see independence and ambition in a woman and they run. Even her dominant boss, Hudson Pierce, has turned down her advances, leaving her to fear that she will never find the lover she's longing for.

Then the most unlikely candidate steps up. Boyd, her much-too-young and oh-so-hot assistant, surprises her one night with bold suggestions and an authoritative demeanor he's never shown her in the office.

It's a bad idea…such a *deliciously bad* idea…but when Boyd takes the reins and leads her to sensual bliss she's never known, the headstrong Norma can't help but fall under his command.

Man in Charge
By Laurelin Paige
Now available.

Scott Sebastian is a rich, cocky playboy. But he's also a romantic who is ready to be everything for the right girl. Has he found her in Tess Turani?

"Oh my God, he was a Sebastian," I repeated to myself."

There are several of them around here," a voice said at my side. An annoyingly delicious and familiar voice. "Dime a dozen."

I turned to find myself face-to-face with the stupid-hot player, and damn if he wasn't even hotter close up.

"You," I said, a bit scornfully because I was feeling contemptuous about the way he lit every nerve in my body on fire. "You," he said in turn. His tone seemed to both appreciate my scorn and know full well the source of it. "I was hoping we'd meet again."

"I was hoping we wouldn't."

"Funny, I don't believe you." He wasn't an idiot, and the truth was glaringly evident. I couldn't stop staring. My eyes were magnetically drawn to him. He was so gorgeous, it made me need to take a seat, and I was already sitting. His hair was lighter, I realized, than I'd figured in the dark. Brownish-red with golden hues, so perfectly messy in distribution that it had to be natural. His eyes were a killer blue. I'd always been a sucker for blue eyes. And for stupid-hot player types. It was like he'd been ordered up for me specifically, a Tessa Turani cocktail guaranteed to make me mind-numbingly drunk from just looking at him.

"Can I buy you a shot?" he asked, as if I needed alcohol when he was in my system.

Somehow I managed to pull my gaze away. "It's an open bar."

"In that case, I can afford to buy you two." He summoned the bartender who hadn't gone far, that nosy little spy. "Four shots of…" Blue Eyes looked at me. "Tequila all right?"

How had he known? "The source of many a bad decision."

"Tequila it is."

He was so smooth. Much smoother than the liquor would be, I knew from experience.

Yet, I didn't object when the bartender put the four shots in front of us, along with a shaker of salt and a bowl of limes.

Just seeing the setup made me want to take my clothes off. Or maybe it was Blue Eyes that did that. He knew how to fill a tux, and I had a feeling he looked even better with it off.

He and the bartender knew exactly where this was going. How dumb was I?

I held up a single shot. "A little obvious, don't you think?"

"That I want to be one of your bad decisions?"

About Laurelin Paige

With millions of books sold, Laurelin Paige is the *NY Times*, *Wall Street Journal*, and *USA Today* Bestselling Author of the Fixed Trilogy. She's a sucker for a good romance and gets giddy anytime there's kissing, much to the embarrassment of her three daughters. Her husband doesn't seem to complain, however. When she isn't reading or writing sexy stories, she's probably singing, watching *Killing Eve* and *Letterkenny,* or dreaming of Michael Fassbender. She's also a proud member of Mensa International though she doesn't do anything with the organization except use it as material for her bio.

You can connect with Laurelin on Facebook at www.facebook.com/LaurelinPaige or on Instagram @thereallaurelinpaige. You can also visit her website, www.laurelinpaige.com, to sign up for e-mails about new releases.

Discover 1001 Dark Nights

COLLECTION ONE

FOREVER WICKED by Shayla Black ~ CRIMSON TWILIGHT by
Heather Graham ~ CAPTURED IN SURRENDER by Liliana Hart ~
SILENT BITE: A SCANGUARDS WEDDING by Tina Folsom ~
DUNGEON GAMES by Lexi Blake ~ AZAGOTH by Larissa Ione ~
NEED YOU NOW by Lisa Renee Jones ~ SHOW ME, BABY by
Cherise Sinclair~ ROPED IN by Lorelei James ~ TEMPTED BY
MIDNIGHT by Lara Adrian ~ THE FLAME by Christopher Rice ~
CARESS OF DARKNESS by Julie Kenner

COLLECTION TWO

WICKED WOLF by Carrie Ann Ryan ~ WHEN IRISH EYES ARE
HAUNTING by Heather Graham ~ EASY WITH YOU by Kristen
Proby ~ MASTER OF FREEDOM by Cherise Sinclair ~ CARESS OF
PLEASURE by Julie Kenner ~ ADORED by Lexi Blake ~ HADES by
Larissa Ione ~ RAVAGED by Elisabeth Naughton ~ DREAM OF YOU
by Jennifer L. Armentrout ~ STRIPPED DOWN by Lorelei James ~
RAGE/KILLIAN by Alexandra Ivy/Laura Wright ~ DRAGON KING
by Donna Grant ~ PURE WICKED by Shayla Black ~ HARD AS
STEEL by Laura Kaye ~ STROKE OF MIDNIGHT by Lara Adrian ~
ALL HALLOWS EVE by Heather Graham ~ KISS THE FLAME by
Christopher Rice~ DARING HER LOVE by Melissa Foster ~ TEASED
by Rebecca Zanetti ~ THE PROMISE OF SURRENDER by Liliana
Hart

COLLECTION THREE

HIDDEN INK by Carrie Ann Ryan ~ BLOOD ON THE BAYOU by
Heather Graham ~ SEARCHING FOR MINE by Jennifer Probst ~
DANCE OF DESIRE by Christopher Rice ~ ROUGH RHYTHM by
Tessa Bailey ~ DEVOTED by Lexi Blake ~ Z by Larissa Ione ~
FALLING UNDER YOU by Laurelin Paige ~ EASY FOR KEEPS by
Kristen Proby ~ UNCHAINED by Elisabeth Naughton ~ HARD TO
SERVE by Laura Kaye ~ DRAGON FEVER by Donna Grant ~
KAYDEN/SIMON by Alexandra Ivy/Laura Wright ~ STRUNG UP by
Lorelei James ~ MIDNIGHT UNTAMED by Lara Adrian ~ TRICKED
by Rebecca Zanetti ~ DIRTY WICKED by Shayla Black ~ THE ONLY
ONE by Lauren Blakely ~ SWEET SURRENDER by Liliana Hart

ABANDON by Rachel Van Dyken ~ THE OPEN DOOR by Laurelin Paige ~ CLOSER by Kylie Scott ~ SOMETHING JUST LIKE THIS by Jennifer Probst ~ BLOOD NIGHT by Heather Graham ~ TWIST OF FATE by Jill Shalvis ~ MORE THAN PLEASURE YOU by Shayla Black ~ WONDER WITH ME by Kristen Proby ~ THE DARKEST ASSASSIN by Gena Showalter

COLLECTION SEVEN
THE BISHOP by Skye Warren ~ TAKEN WITH YOU by Carrie Ann Ryan ~ DRAGON LOST by Donna Grant ~ SEXY LOVE by Carly Phillips ~ PROVOKE by Rachel Van Dyken ~ RAFE by Sawyer Bennett ~ THE NAUGHTY PRINCESS by Claire Contreras ~ THE GRAVEYARD SHIFT by Darynda Jones ~ CHARMED by Lexi Blake ~ SACRIFICE OF DARKNESS by Alexandra Ivy ~ THE QUEEN by Jen Armentrout ~ BEGIN AGAIN by Jennifer Probst ~ VIXEN by Rebecca Zanetti ~ SLASH by Laurelin Paige ~ THE DEAD HEAT OF SUMMER by Heather Graham ~ WILD FIRE by Kristen Ashley ~ MORE THAN PROTECT YOU by Shayla Black ~ LOVE SONG by Kylie Scott ~ CHERISH ME by J. Kenner ~ SHINE WITH ME by Kristen Proby

Discover Blue Box Press
TAME ME by J. Kenner ~ TEMPT ME by J. Kenner ~ DAMIEN by J. Kenner ~ TEASE ME by J. Kenner ~ REAPER by Larissa Ione ~ THE SURRENDER GATE by Christopher Rice ~ SERVICING THE TARGET by Cherise Sinclair ~ THE LAKE OF LEARNING by Steve Berry and M.J. Rose ~ THE MUSEUM OF MYSTERIES by Steve Berry and M.J. Rose ~ TEASE ME by J. Kenner ~ FROM BLOOD AND ASH by Jennifer L. Armentrout ~ QUEEN MOVE by Kennedy Ryan ~ THE HOUSE OF LONG AGO by Steve Berry and M.J. Rose ~ THE BUTTERFLY ROOM by Lucinda Riley ~ A KINGDOM OF FLESH AND FIRE by Jennifer L. Armentrout

On Behalf of 1001 Dark Nights,

Liz Berry, M.J. Rose, and Jillian Stein would like to thank ~

Steve Berry
Doug Scofield
Benjamin Stein
Kim Guidroz
Social Butterfly PR
Ashley Wells
Asha Hossain
Chris Graham
Chelle Olson
Kasi Alexander
Jessica Johns
Dylan Stockton
Richard Blake
and Simon Lipskar

Made in the USA
Las Vegas, NV
16 October 2021